The Cottage

The Cottage

Susan Kay Box Brunner

Published by FWB Publications, Columbus, Ohio.

Published in the United States of America
ISBN: 978-1-940609-79-9
Fiction / Christian / Romance

1

David rose from his midcentury office chair when the ancient grandfather clock chimed. It was now 6:00 p.m. *The men will soon be here.*

In the kitchen, he prepared his famous OJ and then wiggled his long fingers at them. "Work your magic." He had prepared twelve fancy club sandwiches array on their shiny three-tier tray.

A sudden ping sounded on his front door windowpane. David rushed into the living room and pulled opened the door, where he waved to Richard Pair Sr. and Ty Sow. They parked side by side on the circular driveway in front of his suburban home. David called out, "Glad you both could make it." The night air swift in to the house, and it felt warm.

The men nodded back in acknowledgment from their vehicles.

"I hope our card game isn't like the last few month's card games. Nothing against you, Richard Sr., but things have got to change!" David sighed.

Richard Sr.'s deep thundering voice filled the air. His long arms flapped in space, a cell phone pinned under his chin. David shook his head. It was so characteristic of Richard Sr.'s actions when in conversation with a financial client.

At the slamming sound, David shifted his eyes. Ty had kicked the driver's door of his twenty-year-old station wagon shut.

David stepped aside, and let his old school friends enter the house.

Ty said, "Just look at the card table. David, you've thought of everything." Then pointing, he continued, "Score sheets, pencils, and a new deck of sealed cards."

David folded his arms across his chest. His smile deepened.

The three men sat at their regular positions. Richard Sr. wiggled his eyebrows and began to shuffle. He dealt seven cards to each player. Then he knocked on the card table. David and Ty immediately glanced each other's way. Richard Sr. belted, "Beat these beauties!"

David and Ty bit their bottom lip and just shook their head.

Ty shuffled, then dealt the cards. David caught a twinkle in Ty's eyes. But Richard Sr. quickly knocked on the table, "I'll pass."

Ty moaned, then stretched his hands out, folding his cards again. David dealt. The room quieted. The other two men gave a knock on the table, but David moaned, "I'll take two cards."

All eyes shifted on Ty. He licked his lips and guffawed as he laid down his cards. David waved his hand and laid down his cards, beaming. Then Richard Sr. rose to his feet and did a victory dance. Unfortunately, again Richard Sr.'s hand had trumped Ty and David's hand. David scooted from his chair, shook his head, and rolled his brown eyes. He held the pitcher high. "Anyone for juice?"

The men saluted, and David poured the freshly squeezed orange juice laced with homemade vanilla ice cream, and then he placed a peppermint leaf at the side of their glass.

Richard Sr. said, "David, I don't want a leaf. Hogwash!"

"The peppermint leaf cleans your pilot," David replied.

Ty took another sip, then said, "Your signature drink is the requested drink throughout Virginia. And is catered at almost every event."

"Are you keeping the sandwiches for yourself?" Richard Sr. thundered.

David lifted the platter of club sandwiches and laughed.

"Are we ready to play another hand?" Richard Sr. was shuffling the cards.

David and Ty held their breath as the cards were dealt. David hung his head, laying his cards down, and Ty followed . "Are you both folding, again?" His hands were up in the air.

Ty pinched his nose. "David, it looks like we've lost in cards again." Moaning.

Richard Sr. voice was earsplitting as he claimed, "Another victory!"

David walked into the kitchen, and the men soon followed with conversation. Ty, in his quiet manner, said, "I wish Jathrow and Vivian were here. We five used to have so much fun."

The room stilled, and feet shifted. David cleared his throat. "Speaking of Jathrow, has anyone heard from him lately?"

Richard Sr. reached for another sandwich. "Funny you should ask. I heard from Jathrow Mowey just this morning. In fact, he chatted about sunny California and his surfing. He implied life on the beach was anything but tiring, saying, 'It's fun watching all the Sun Bunnies.'"

David raked his unmanageable red hair. "He usually calls me every month."

Richard Sr. tapped his glass, holding it out for more juice. "You know Jathrow. He's still the same old friend through and through." Richard Sr.'s lips thinned. "He called Vivian's cell phone. He found out the number had been disconnected. Then he mentioned his stay last spring with Dr. Keith Rose and Vivian, you know, because all motels and hotels were filled during the annual Attorney's Fundraising Convention. And that was the purpose of his call."

"Well, Jathrow is peculiar." David washed the glasses and plates, then said, "Did you see Jathrow's pictures in our last week's paper? I think his state's paper, *California News*, and the *GQ* magazine reported coverage. Anyway, the article read, 'Jathrow Mowey number one again on the most eligible bachelors list. And still remains untamed by any female!'"

Ty grunted. "Whenever Jathrow is on TV, radio, or is featured in magazines, he's photographed with a different striking-looking woman. I think his lifestyle would get old!"

David hunched his shoulders while drying his hands. "Just saying, Jathrow's photos shows off his physique." David hung the drying towel over the sink. "I think his shirtless poses are way too much."

Jathrow is over six feet with shoulder-length blond hair. Richard Sr. belched and brought his glass to the sink.

Ty said, "Now let's be fair about our friend. He's intellectual, and he's not all play. The last article I read stated, 'Jathrow Mowey, ranked number one attorney in the USA—Divorce Specialist.' We all know he graduated from UC Berkeley School of Law and has practiced law for thirty-four years."

David nodded.

"People around the world, seek out Jathrow's law services, you see this in the papers all the time, Hollywood's so-so represented by our Jathrow, He's famous," said Richard Sr..

"I'm sure Jathrow is still satisfied being a confirmed bachelor. And is more set in his ways than ever."

Ty sighed and said, "Especially with Jathrow being so rich and powerful."

David frowned. "We shouldn't be surprised. We knew his goals way back in high school, 1959." He poked Richard Sr. "Remember our graduation night?" Jathrow had claimed he would never marry, but he looked straight at Vivian and flashed his piercing blue eyes. Then Jathrow slid into a cab, rolled down a window, and screamed, "California, here I come!" And he mouthed, "David, I wish you and Doreen all life's best. She's a peach." And he winked.

"As I recall we all stood there in awe well after the cab's tail lights had vanished from sight, said David."

Richard Sr. walked over to the mantle and traced the gold-framed black-and-white high school photo of the five of them standing arm in arm. Looking up, he asked, "Wasn't this the night of our senior prom? We were ready to face the world head-on."

David nodded. "So much time has passed, and look how far we have come."

A door slammed, and David heard Doreen's voice. She was his wife of thirty-five years.

Doreen walked through the kitchen and breathlessly called, "Honey, I'm home!"

Ty and Richard Sr. stepped forward, and each gave Doreen a friendly hug. David bent and kissed her plump cheek. He moved backward, holding his chest, and gasped, "Did you buy out Tyson's Corner?"

Doreen blushed from her husband's words and adjusted her shoulders, and mumbled, "Men." She looked in Ty's direction. "Did you lose at cards again?" Doreen tilted her head. "Who kept score? Did Richard Sr. win again?"

Ty cleared his throat and, in his quiet manner, said, "Mrs. Fleck, David and I lost again." His lips twitched before adding, "Just look at Richard Sr.'s face. Doesn't it tell all? He's smiling like a Cheshire cat and patting his fat wallet."

Richard Sr.'s gray eyes widened. "Now, Mrs. Fleck, we never play for money." He scratched his balding head. "It wouldn't be the Christian thing to do."

Doreen set her packages down and lifted a chubby finger. "For the record, your wives and I shopped at Tyson's Corner today, and we shopped and ate dinner." She grabbed the handles of her bags. The only sounds heard were the swishing of packages and her three-inch heels clicking down the hall toward the bedroom.

David chuckled at his wife's sense of humor, but Ty's jaw drop. It was open knowledge that Ty's wife was not working and their sole livelihood was in Ty's cleaning business. David looked over at Richard Sr. and said, "I'm glad you keep Ty and I abreast of the community comings and goings. This information helps both Ty and I in our business."

Richard Sr. had taken over his father's business, which was called Pair's Financial twenty-three years ago and had offered sound business advice, which launched the financial company into the twentieth century.

Ty and Richard Sr. walked to the coat rack, and David went to the front door and thanked each of his friends for coming. And said a silent prayer for the friendship of his fellowmen, before projecting his voice, "Richard Sr., did Jathrow say if he would be back in Virginia again this year?"

Richard Sr. twirled his hat, pouted his lips, and answered, "Come to think of it, no. But I gave him Vivian's new cell number."

Ty walked out behind Richard Sr. and waved a hand when he reached his station wagon. Richard Sr. shouted over his Cadillac motor, "Ty, will your schedule allow you to add on another commercial cleaning?"

"Sure. When?"

Richard Sr. reached for his ringing cell phone and projected his voice before answering his call, "I'll text you."

The door closed behind David as he stepped onto the front porch. The only sound heard was from the crickets. He folded into a rocking chair, and an unexpected breeze crossed his face. *The weather feels wickedly good.*

Gazing into the sky, he watched the sun fade into streaks of orange, pink, and purple. Vivian came to mind. He missed their weekly conversations, and when had they last seen each other?

It was at the doctor's wake. He had walked into the doctor's galley kitchen to pour out the leftover juice, only to be surprised by a heated conversation, which exploded between Vivian and her daughter. He heard Vivian's pleading voice saying, "Jacey Rose, try and understand why I must sell Dr. Rose's house. He's no longer alive, you refused this house, and I'll be moving to the cottage."

Jacey had stomped away.

David cleared his throat and continued his work. He remembered how Vivian enjoyed her visits at the quaint cottage with all its surrounding natural beauty of English flower gardens and the private beach she found across the cottage's hidden pathway. Vivian spent hours, weeks, even months there working on her novels.

I should call Vivian. Vivian has a new released novel party coming up. Then he recalled that her agent made all the arrangements. David sat down. He fingered the signed copy of Vivian's tenth novel, *The Key*. It was couriered to his house. David owned Vivian's entire book series. She has a true flare in mystical writings.

The door squeaked, and Doreen stepped onto the front porch. "Honey, is everything all right? You seem quiet tonight." She smiled. "Here, I brought you a decaf ."

David stood. "Thanks, sweetheart." He reached for the cup of hot liquid, and as his eyes crinkled, he said, "Everything is fine, especially since you're here." David nuzzled her neck with tiny kisses. Doreen giggled and edged closer placing a hand on his chest. He set the cup down and locked eyes with her. She edged her soft fingers through his thick dark red mane. David nibbled her ear and whispered, "I love you more today than yesterday."

Doreen shivered as he lowered his head, claiming her mouth. He stepped back, still holding her, and said, "I've never regretted us marrying while we were so young. Except, Doreen, sadness does fill my heart, for it was years before you could fulfill your educational dream." They remained silent, entwined in each other's arms.

They were just seventeen. He was amazed they graduated from high school that June. David had embarked in a new business career, catering. Within a few working weeks, his business showed great potential.

Doreen had become his wife and a mother. She had blossomed overnight from her young youth into adulthood and gave birth to their only daughter, Dee Dee. He had been scared, thrilled, and astonished when Doreen revealed her pregnancy. With in the week they stood before a justice of peace and pledged their eternal vows. Their witnesses were their best school buddies, Richard Sr., Ty, and Vivian. All were sad Jathrow could not attend as he was in California.

The night air carried Doreen's heavenly scent, and it wavered under David's nose. He tightened his grip around her. He sat down and pulled her onto his lap and began rocking. He leaned his head against hers. David's throat thickened as he recalled their past.

Doreen's parents never accepted their marriage. Instead, they shunned her and had abruptly moved away. Doreen never had the opportunity to share any news of her pregnancy and their now grown granddaughter.

After several months of marriage, David recalled a deep emptiness stirred within him. A client had mentioned to him of an outdoor old-fashioned revival tent meeting, which was at the edge of town. At that moment, he made a decision for Doreen and him to attend. .

Doreen adjusted her dress and settled into his chest. David shuddered as his mind drifted to the dreadful day he was summoned to the principal's office in high school.

❧❀☙

Ms. Barnes was a matter-of-fact creature whose voice was chilling and when she delivered her words, he'd feel like she breathed ice over his form.

Ms. Barnes looked away from him. "There's been a horrible car accident that happened a few miles out of town." She glanced David's way. And like a stone statue, she said, "I'm sorry, but both your parents were killed outright. And so was the driver of the other car. My assistant and school's councilor, Bill Knapp, will provide help in anyway and drive you home when you are ready." Ms. Barnes left the room, squaring her spinster shoulders.

The ride to his house was in silence. David refused any further help from Mr. Knapp and slid from his car muttering, "Thank you." David called no one about the tragedy. A deep inner darkness gripped him. Later in the day, his friends rushed to his side, but he turned them away. There was no relief for his grief, and he was not yet a spiritual man.

The town's funeral director on behalf of the high school's councilor called David and made arrangements. Doreen became his angel of mercy. She showered him with love, understanding, and comfort before and after school. The following month, she spoke with him about their baby. Marriage wasn't an issue. He had been taught as a youth how real men step up to the plate.

❧❧❧

David felt Doreen's warm lips, and he patted her arm. He reached for his cold coffee. The evening's darkness had come as the clouds covered the heavens. Only a quarter moon managed to escape the clouds and shine through.

David said, "My dear, let's call it a day." A smile lifted the corners of his mouth, and hand in hand, they walked into the house. David closed the door with his foot and set the empty cup down. He whistled and slapped her bottom, saying, "Woman, come here!" He carried her into the bedroom and released her.

She gave him a quick kiss, giggled, and answered, "I'll only be a moment."

David found matches and lit scented candles. He lifted the silk sheet and slid between the cool layers. The faithful sound of the urban bed squeaked. He said, "I'm waiting."

2

The early morning's bright sun peered through the east window and woke David. Although still tired, he pushed himself up and made the telephone call to Ty. He needed to confirm his help for Vivian's upcoming gala to be held at the cottage. He regretted not mentioning the event to Ty while they were playing cards.

"Ty Sow here."

"This is David. Sorry it's so early, but I'm calling you about Vivian's upcoming novel release party. Was wondering if you are available to help out with serving?"

"Well, good morning to you too, David! When's the event?"

"I need to call Mr. Gee first and reaffirm the date and time. Can I call you later today?"

"Count me in, David. This is my slow time of the year." The line went dead.

Mr. Samuel Gee was called, and the date and time was confirmed. Then David dialed Ty back and waited.

Ty was out of breath. "Is the event a go? And when and time, please?"

David yawned again. "It is two weeks from Thursday, an all-afternoon-and-evening affair. At the luncheon, we serve hors d'oeuvre, artichokes, anchovies, cheese and crackers, along with assorted fruits. The drinks served will be hot brewed tea and iced, and my OJ specialty. At the five o'clock dinner, we change into black-tie dress code. Mr. Samuel Gee said Vivian wants her guest be offered a choice, split pea or onion soup topped with cheese. Then we'll serve a chef's salad. Half an hour later, we'll serve meat platters of filet mignon and stuffed chicken breast. Other servers will handle the vegetables trays and baskets of rolls."

"The meal sounds a lot like the menu you served at my fourth daughter's wedding reception a few months ago." He muttered, "I had to use my rainy-day fund again. My baby girl Sybil just wouldn't wait until spring to wed the man of her dreams. Women!"

"Thanks for your help, Ty. You're a great friend. Good-bye."

David rubbed his eyes and punched in Richard Sr.'s cell number. Richard Sr.'s answering service said, "Leave a brief message, and I'll get back with you."

David's phone beeped, signaling an incoming call. The screen displayed "Vivian Rose."

"Hello, Mrs. Rose. Is everything all right?"

Vivian chuckled. "David, David. After all these years, you know better than to call me by my formal name! Now the reason why I've called, I want to add four additional straight back chairs with the blush pink satin ribbon ties to place on the front lawn near my door entrance. In case some people want to sit outside and view the gardens. David, be at the cottage tomorrow morning, ten o'clock."

"I'll be there."

"Sorry, must go. Jacey is beeping through."

David rushed. "Will Jacey be in town for your party?"

"No, she's in Australia, filmmaking. See you tomorrow."

David closed his cell phone lid, then put the phone back in his shirt pocket.

At exactly 10:00 a.m., he arrived at Vivian's to go over the final food list, entertainment, and sitting arrangements of the people and to assured her that the chairs were ordered.

Two weeks passed, and the magical day for Vivian's book party arrived.

News of her new novel carried in their local and state paper. Also posted was to RSVP if attending.

David walked into the hallway where Mr. Samuel Gee stood talking on his cell phone. He checked the flower arrangement for their freshness and inhaled the pleasant aroma of the long-stemmed pink roses. David noticed Vivian through the wall mirror. She appeared a little nervous as she lifted a hand to her red hair. She feathered unseen strands into the eloquent low-sitting bun at the back of her neck. David admired her strength and beauty.

Her flittering socialite agent, Samuel Gee, squared his shoulders after closing up his phone and handed David a clipboard.

With raised eyebrows, he asked, "What's this for?"

"A guest list. I need to know who attends this party."

David walked through each room, pausing, as he checked the guest list. He spoke in passing through the large crowd. All guests were accounted for except one, Jathrow Mowey.

Ty lift his hand and caught David's eye. He motioned to the house phone. David nodded and edged through the crowd over to Vivian. In a low voice, he said, "You have a call waiting on the house phone."

In the privacy of her bedroom, Vivian pushed speaker button on the phone and turned the volume low. "This is Vivian Rose."

David, who was standing near, heard, "Hello, Mother, I called to wish you well. How's the party?"

"Jacey, you know Mr. Gee is a whiz at these social events, but it does amaze me every time how my novel sells." Vivian sighed. "I need more books printed. They've sold out."

"Mom, I hear edginess in your voice." She hesitated. "Is it because father is not with you?"

"Oh, Jacey, I'm sorry, but no! This isn't about your father." She blew out a breath. "I spotted a photographer snooping around the cottage yesterday. He snapped pictures and rummaged though the trash. I really don't need his kind of publicity."

"How awful. Are you safe? Did you call the police?"

Vivian heard concern in her daughter's voice. "No. But I did let Mr. Samuel Gee know. And he is all over it. Also, I've decided to rent out one of my rooms. Now don't worry. We'll talk later."

"Ah, I must hurry. They're calling me for filmmaking. Bye."

At 10:00 p.m., the book party was over, and Vivian floated on cloud nine as her agent applauded her. Samuel Gee said, "You've done it again. Another best seller, and what a successful party."

Vivian rolled her green eyes. "Thanks, Sam, couldn't have done it without you." She glanced around the room. "Has everyone left?"

"Almost," he answered. "David and Ty are finishing up in the kitchen. And waiting for the floras to be pickup and delivered at the town's senior center."

Vivian glanced outside and saw Ty anchoring the china dishes on the catering truck. David was placing the not-so-white linens in their bins. Vivian opened the door and clapped her hands. "Thanks for another great service. Come, collect your checks."

David stepped on the front porch. Vivian touched his arm and said, "Friends after so many years. David, do you remember how surprised I was to find out you catered for Dr. Rose?" She giggled.

David leaned back on his heels, folded his arms, and said, "I do indeed." The late Dr. Keith Rose was a very respected individual, as a man, and in his professional realm. He was also generous. "It was my privilege to serve him all those years. Dr. Keith Rose gave me my first real break in catering. He will be missed by all." David saw moistness around Vivian's eyes. He handed her a handkerchief. "I thought the doctor was a confirmed bachelor, until you two became engaged. I was flabbergasted when I heard the news. He was so much older than you." He sighed. "My Doreen always assumed you and Jathrow would be the couple."

Vivian dabbed her eyes and her lower lip quivered.

"Your husband entertained a lot. And from my observation, he didn't enjoy or relax at the parties. But the guests never seemed to notice."

Vivian drew in a breath. "Keith was from a very old traditional and established family, which held prestige in their community. He was wealthy, by inheritance, and by his work rights. When his medical findings were published, his shyness worsened. Dr. Rose wasn't about fame. He was a dedicated doctor who liked helping people with their health issues." She took a step and paused. "He was a caring man and a fine husband. I wouldn't have Jacey if it were not for him. We did have our ups and downs though." She blew her nose. "He could be like an old mule." Vivian's voice trailed. "Dr. Rose didn't understand the filmmaking business. And he was dead set against Jacey's acting. He wanted her to become a doctor as he." Her green eyes widened. "Oh, David, I've said too much!"

David patted Vivian's hand.

Ty coughed and asked, "Is there anything else we can do for you, Vivian, dear?"

Vivian scanned the rooms, then said, "No, my friends, everything was perfect." She handed Ty his check.

Ty nodded. "Thank you." He smiled.

An unexpected noise filtered through the front door's screen window. Vivian jumped. Ty motioned to David and silently counted to three on his fingers. David nodded and headed out the front door leaving Vivian inside the cottage. Ty went out the back door and slid around toward the front. Ty screamed, "I got him!"

"Great." David answered as he made quick steps.

Starring down at the captured victim, he asked, "Richard Pair Sr., what are you doing back here at the cottage?"

The screen door creaked open, and Vivian marched outside. She seized Richard's earlobe and echoed, "Well answer."

His face reddened as it did when he was a teen, and he stuttered, "I-I received a phone call from Jathrow. He didn't seem to know anything about Dr. Keith Rose's passing. He promised to call you, Vivian. He wants to rent a room from you again this year."

Vivian puffed, "Why didn't you just call?"

Richard Sr. lowered his booming voice. "You know I felt bad for leaving the party earlier, but I had to attend to personal business. After I finished with my client, I thought you would want to know Jathrow called. Do you have any OJ left?"

Just then, Richard Sr.'s cell phone rang. The ringtone was "Lion Sleeps Tonight." The redness in Richard Sr.'s face deepened. "Chloe changed the ringer!" he moaned. "Hello, this is Richard Pair Sr." He took a few steps and composed himself. "How may I help you?" His eyebrows arched, "Jathrow Mowey!" Richard Sr. turned and walked to Vivian and gave Vivian his cell phone. "It's Jathrow."

The three men stared in disbelief as a sweet smile spread from Vivian's lips.

"I wonder why Jathrow didn't call her directly. Didn't you say you gave him Vivian's number?" David inquired.

Richard Sr. shrugged. "I honestly don't know why he didn't call her directly. Unless Jathrow was hesitant after hearing about her husband's death," Richard Sr. rubbed his chin. "Although Jathrow asked a strange question. He asked if I knew of any available intelligent single women here."

David questioned, "Why?"

"Jathrow said he needed a date for the upcoming Attorney Action Fundraiser. He was chuckling the whole time and then quite soberly said, 'I'm tired of being with bimbos.'"

Vivian nudged Richard Sr. and handed him his cell phone. She glanced at the three men. "Jathrow will be here next weekend, and yes, I've rented him a room." She tapped David on the chest. "We need a welcome home party for our friend. Let's keep it low-key for Jathrow. We'll invite your wives and add a few single women to the mix to balance out the party. David, you'll need to be here tomorrow morning, say, ten o'clock." Vivian turned and without a word walked inside the cottage. Through the screen door, she shouted, "Goodnight, gentlemen."

❧

The sound of rushing waves crashing on the beach woke Vivian the next morning. She remembered she left the bedroom window open before she retired for bed.

She made her way to the kitchen and brewed a black-orange tea. Opening the front door, Vivian held a cup of brewed tea, and sat on the porch. She took in a breath of fresh air. *I've loved this cottage from the time I laid my eyes on it. Hmm. What a surprise it was when I stumbled upon the hidden cottage. If it hadn't been for the old dust-covered sign with an arrow pointing south, my, my.*

She had followed the wooded path, and then the bungalow came into view. She gasped and touched the faded rail, admiring the weather-beaten wraparound front porch. She momentarily looked at the unkempt gardens and the surrounding forest which led into the mountain foothills. Vivian rubbed her eyes in disbelief, seeing a For Sale sign taped on the front bay window. She took her sleeve and rubbed the dust from the windowpane, seeing the cottage was empty seemingly neglected for years. The cottage begged for her attention. She backed down the porch steps and walked to the edge of the front yard. Vivian kicked the drifted white sand, and a walkway was exposed. She followed the path and paused as a beautiful private beach was revealed. She slipped off her shoes and let the warm ooze of sand gush between her toes. Vivian inhaled and exhaled. She felt at home and was determined to own the cottage at any price.

She had gone back to the mansion and let her news of the cottage come gushing out to her husband. She clapped her hands in glee about her found treasure.

Unfortunately Dr. Keith Rose hadn't understood her need, and she couldn't explain. It led to their first and only horrible quarrel . He insisted she pass on the sale. He offered her the use of any room in his traditional house for an office. He invited her to decorate it to her satisfaction, but Vivian remained stubborn and expressed she didn't want to be obligated. She shivered at the thought of his cold, eerie house and was overwhelmed with its starchiness. The spent weeks debating about this, and finally the doctor approved the purchase.

Vivian spent every opportunity at the cottage decorating and painting it to her satisfaction. She made the rooms bright, airy, and cozy. Her husband rarely made his presence felt at the cottage unless Vivian hosted a novel release party. The doctor would attend and supported her as a loyal husband. She was forever grateful to him.

She was brought back from her musing by a flock of birds flying overhead; Vivian glanced toward the sun. It was promising. She went inside and changed into work attire. Then grabbed her gloves and placed on the pink floppy hat. At the shed, she flipped on the light and squinted. Vivian wheeled the tool cart into the front yard where the late roses were still in bloom. The aroma captivated her. She shook her head as she recalled that when she first arrived at the cottage, the roses looked pathetic among all the weeds. She pulled the long-nose pruning shears from the cart and began grooming the climbers. Vivian worked relentlessly, for sixty minutes, and stood with sweat beads on her brow. Reaching for bottled water, she felt the sun's rays rapidly rising. She heard the sound of gravel and saw David's catering truck rolling onto the driveway. He carried a clipboard and was whistling. She wondered what suggestions he would have for Jathrow's party. She felt heaviness in her soul but didn't understand why.

"Hello, Vivian." He tipped his hat and dusted off his boots. "Isn't it a beautiful morning? And I see you've been busy. Your place is looking great!"

"Thanks." She nodded.

"Are you ready to check over the party plans?"

"I am." Vivian smiled while removing her gloves. She motioned for them to sit on the porch. "Go ahead. Fill me in on your ideas."

He handed over the clipboard as he spoke, "I think the welcome-back party for Jathrow should be an outdoor barbecue." He watched for Vivian's reactions.

She clapped with satisfaction.

Then David suggested adding a country band. They decided on a time and date for the party. David left with all the instructions and waved good-bye from the catering truck.

Vivian slugged down another cold drink before carrying a flat of wilted white daisies to add to the side flowerbed. Her stomach rolled and gave off a loud grumble. She noticed the country sundial had changed positions, showing it was well past noon. It was time for lunch. Vivian washed and prepared a cucumber sandwich and poured a glass of iced tea. After a few sips, she propped her feet up, muttering, "I'll close my eyes for a moment."

Vivian woke with the pink floppy hat lodged at the side of her face. Glancing at the clock, she saw it was now two hours later. She reached for the lopsided hat and plopped it back on her head. In the yard, she reached for the rake as she worked her way in the flowerbed. Vivian admired all the hard labor where daisies were surrounded by lavender bushes and lovely pink roses. She breathed deeply and smiled.

3

The winds shifted, causing a sage of wonderful fragrance to filter through the air. Vivian lifted her head, welcoming another breeze. When the familiar scent of wood musk of a man drifted under her nose, she whirled, stumbled, and her stomach tied in knots. "Jathrow!"

He was a week early. He walked down the sandy path, toting a large suitcase. She took quick breaths struggling to gain control. Just the sight of his sun-bleached hair blowing in the wind made her dizzy. His Linnet jacket was slung over his shoulder. His silk shirt stood open, displaying the flat bronze bareness to the waist. She willed her feet still. Excitement and warmth flooded over her, which she hadn't experience since Jathrow left Virginia State, right after high school. Vivian gave herself a quick lecture, "It's just Jathrow, my handsome friend from high school." She squared her shoulders.

He dropped the suitcase and ran to her. He swung Vivian around until they both laughed. Jathrow said, "Congratulations on your new book, Viv. I brought a copy with me for you to sign." He looked into Vivian's round green eyes; then the smile faded and was replaced by a sober sorrowful expression.

Vivian's eyes widened as Jathrow caught his breath.

He stepped nearer and spoke his regret and sorrow about her deceased husband, Dr. Keith Rose. There was stillness in the air. He wrapped his arms around her to comfort. Then he lowered his head and his lips touched Vivian's lips in a slow way.

Vivian raised her arms and twined them around his neck. She edged closer, breathing in his scent. On tiptoe, she returned his lingering kiss.

Jathrow made a sudden movement from Vivian. He shook his head and grabbed the suitcase. He voiced hurriedly, "Viv, I'm sorry I've overstepped, but how I've missed you!" He took another step away from her, biting his bottom full lip.

She shuddered, perplexed. She removed her hat. "What a sight I must be. Come on in, and I'll show you to your room." A nervous giggle slipped. "Are you hungry?" Her stomach churned as he walked nearer.

"I am hungry, but after unpacking, I'd like to go for a swim. You know me and water."

"All right, your meal will be left in the oven on warm. Help yourself when you're ready. Have fun at the beach. The water is perfect this time of day."

Jathrow nodded and continued his walk into the rented bedroom. He leaned against the closed door, blew out a held breath, then said, "Wow, that kiss from her was unexpected. Nice." He shivered. "Wrong, Jathrow. She just lost her husband."

Vivian called David from her cell phone and left him a message. "I'm on my way to your house. Jathrow is here at the cottage. We need to bump up his welcome home party to this weekend."

❧❦❧

After finalizing the party plans, she then visited with Doreen, giving her a hug. She talked about the weather and its warmth for the time of year and her new book release.

Doreen said, "I can't hardly wait until your book event party. I love the socializing and hearing praise of your success, and smiled. Tell me Vivian, how's your English flower gardens this time of the year?"

Vivian replied, "Oh thanks for the support," and touched her arm. She continued, "The flowers are planted and the roses all pruned. Thanks for asking."

Farewells were made.

❧❦❧

After leaving David's place, Vivian drove her ford truck into town. A sign outside a salon said, Walks-Ins Welcome at Cut and Curl. Vivian treated herself to a long overdue cut and wash. The operator suggested a nail enhancement and pedicure of polished apple red. Afterward she walked on Main Street and spotted a bright-colored dress on display. Vivian rushed inside the store and asked for the dress. Vivian found it to be formfitting. She instantly bought it. She selected red sandals and a red wide-brim hat to perfect the outfit for Friday's "Welcome Home, Jathrow" barbecue. She glanced at the sky; the sun was setting, and the night air was crisp.

When she arrived home, Jathrow appeared on the porch wearing shorts and a tight-fitting polo shirt. He carried iced tea and handed a glass to Vivian, before sitting on the porch steps.

The sounds of the beach came from across the road.

His blue eyes were lowered as he distanced himself from Vivian.

A few nights passed since they kissed, and Jathrow regained his nerve to inquire, "Viv, how have things been since your husband died?"

"Busy." Vivian sipped her nightly tea. Seconds past. "Clearing out Keith's books, clothing, and furniture was hard, but dealing with his medical equipment was heart wrenching." Vivian stood stretching. "Selling the big house was effortless for me. I never enjoyed his mansion much after I lived there. It was dark, formal, and there were way too many servants. And all those stairs to climb." She shuddered. "To me, the mansion held a cold stuffy eerie feeling." Vivian glanced at Jathrow and held his gaze. "It was only a month after Keith died that one of his doctor friends called out of the blue and made me an offer on the mansion. I could not refuse. And he kept on all the help for which I was grateful."

Jathrow stood with eyes squinted, "I read about Dr. Rose's medical publishing. What an impressive man!" Jathrow paced and turned, locking eyes with Vivian. "I called Richard Sr. and David the day before you married him. They informed me Dr. Keith Rose treasured you. That he was kind and a very generous man when it came to you." He held up his hand to silence her. "Viv, I'm glad you moved on with your life and didn't wait for me to come back." He shrugged. "I thought about you wanting me to stay in Virginia with you while in our teen years." He shifted. "And I questioned myself again after college graduation on rather there could ever be an…us. Matter of fact, Viv, I thought about you and me the entire time I've lived in California. I just wasn't sure we could ever be more than friends."

Vivian stomped her foot. She opened the screen door and yelled, "I did wait for you for twelve years, Jathrow Mowey. But when you didn't bother to answer my letters and even returned some letter to me, unopened, trust me, I moved on with my life!" Pointing her finger, she said, "Let me assure you I was young then. And it was a long, long time ago." Seconds passed, then the cottage door slammed. However after a few seconds, Vivian passed by Jathrow, who was still standing there where she left him. "I'm going swimming."

She glanced over her shoulder; Jathrow's mouth was gaped open.

Jathrow's Adam apple bobbed. He realized Vivian had waited for him. Had she wanted more than friendship? Would she give him a second chance now, being they were older? His stomach rolled. He watched, unable to move as Vivian ran down the sandy path heading for the water. She flipped on her back and stroked out in the lake. She was almost out of sight.

Jathrow ran and tugged at his tight-fitting polo and flung it to the side. He shimmied from his shorts, leaving on his skinny blue briefs. The water was cold, but Jathrow pushed toward her. Her magnificent strokes magnetically pulled him to her. With each stroke, he struggled with his own thoughts. *I've always preferred younger, blonder, taller, slimmer women.* Jathrow swam harder. *Vivian doesn't fit my image of women, and she certainly isn't petite.* He half smiled. *Vivian is indeed a full-figured woman, coupled with spice and completed with sweetness.* Didn't he say to Richard Sr. he wanted a warm, saucy, educated woman.? He stopped and treaded water. Vivian's face appeared with her soft warm inviting lips. He realized he wanted her. He reached her, and they touched. Vivian moved like lighting had struck her. With force and ambition, he swam toward her again. Vivian was in trouble. She had swum out too far. Jathrow's arms made deeper strokes, but she became helpless. Vivian gulped water and went under. Her head bobbed under a second time. Jathrow swam harder and pushed himself to the limit.

Vivian realized she was in danger and just not from Jathrow. She became dizzy. Her arms and legs were heavy. *I'm drowning.* Darkness drifted near and then out-and-out darkness.

The next thing Vivian experienced was warmth on her mouth and grittiness on her back. She blinked and blinked again. Focusing in, she found herself staring back into Jathrow's warm sea-blue eyes. Even coughing and spitting up water, Vivian knew she was safe, for his arms held her close. She could hear his heart beating. He rocked her back and forth before lifting her up. The last thing she heard was his soothing words of endearment, "My Viv," and it filled her soul.

Vivian woke up with the sun's brightness and warmth peeking through her bedroom bay window. Looking under the sheet, Vivian saw she wasn't wearing much. With one eye opened, she bobbed her head from the covers and appreciated that no one else was in her bed or in the room. She breathed a sigh of relief (or was it regret?). She filled her lungs with air and prayed, "Thank you, Jesus, for saving me." She asked forgiveness for sinful thoughts as she encountered visions of muscular Jathrow. Grabbing her bright pink fluffy robe, she gathered it and slipped on her matching fuzzy house shoes. Heading into the kitchen, she saw a note pinned on the wall over the coffee maker.

> Vivian, had business in town. Thankful that your breathing became steady and even. You're still gorgeous! Perfect body. Thanks for the image. Hope you had enough covers. Oh, I am looking forward to the surprise party tonight. I heard about the women. Signed: L., Jathrow.

Vivian felt heated and was all shades of red. Questions ran through her mind. *Did he undress me?* She shook her head. No, Jathrow was teasing her like he always had. She shifted from one foot to the other while making tea. When the phone rang, Vivian jumped. "Hello?"

"Vivian," David spoke. "The band will arrive at 5:30 p.m. sharp and at six I'll be bringing the food. The chicken and ribs have been marinating since last night. Ty and Richard Sr. should be there soon after to arrange the outside kitchen. I thought with the open bar we would serve soft drinks, my specialty juice, and bottled water if you agree." He paused. "Did I mention the tables and chairs are to arrive at four and I have their denim coverings? Say, are you ready for some down home fun?"

Vivian said, "David, all sounds fine, and I'm getting there." She clucked and asked, "What about the women? Did you find a few lucky volunteers?"

A sick laugh escape. She knew women would not be a problem. Her stomach rolled. What was it about Jathrow after all these years?

"Doreen did. She asked the librarian, Jill Monroe, and Betty Jane, the nurse from our new medical center, and for fun, she included crazy, funny Kate Kit, from the restaurant. All will meet Jathrow's expectation, interest, and liking."

"David, aren't they a little young?"

"No. One of the ladies is your age, and the other two ladies are just a few years younger than you, Vivian. Well, I've got to go. My other line is beeping. See you soon."

Vivian scooted the kitchen chair and didn't care if it screeched.

She mocked, "'Only a little younger than you are.' So what's wrong with me?" She fluffed her red cropped hair and flopped down into a chair. She closed her eyes, crossed her arms, but it wasn't Jathrow who came to mind.

❧❀❧

It was autumn and after her graduation from business school. A call from her mother requested her to come home. Carol Litten was a retired educator and was born with a hearing impairment and developed MS. Vivian learned sign language at an early age.

Every week after moving back home, she drove her mother to Dr. Keith Rose's office. She had regular check up and blood draws. Carol insisted being dropped off near the doctor's front door, leaving Vivian to run household errands or visit the library.

After months, her mother passed away. Vivian became the executor of Carol's estate. Two weeks following the funeral, Vivian drove the Century Buick, which her mother had willed her, to town. She collected the coroner's report for bills and insurance purposes. Dr. Keith Rose had asked her to come into his office with the paperwork.

When she arrived, there was no room to sit. The doctor's waiting area was narrow and full of patients. The office phone was ringing wildly. Babies were screaming, and the whole room was in chaos. Vivian approached the mammoth walnut desk and looked for a sign-in sheet. She found charts laying everywhere, irregularly stacked, and blank forms were scattered. There wasn't a receptionist in sight and no sign-in sheet. She felt a breeze on her legs when a side door opened. A very tall, slender silver-haired man with eyes of steel blue appeared in a white flapping coat. He said to her, "Miss, thanks for coming in so quickly. Will you just answer the phone!" His eyes appeared like flaming fiery darts and his nostrils flared. He stared at her demanding obedience.

So she scanned the waiting room and anxiously looked for the individual who was to come forward. Who could he possibly be addressing? She glanced his way and swallowed, "Me?"

Vivian gawked when the doctor pointed his long index finger at her and yelled, "Answer the phone!

She edged backward, reaching the desk, and set her purse and her mother's file down. In a whisper, Vivian said, "Doctor Rose's office. Can I help you?"

The woman at the other end nonstop rattled, "I'm late for my morning's appointment. I'll be there in twenty minutes."

Vivian gained composure. She asked the woman, "Your name, please?"

But the phone line silence. She stared at the receiver. It rang again. She grabbed the receiver, "Hello, Doctor Rose's Office, and who's calling? Miss, excuse me! Please stop talking. Now that your name is written down, I need a phone number for you to be called back for a doctor's appointment." She listened and after a while, she said, "Thank you for calling." She hesitated before placing the receiver down. She listened; the phone remained silent. She breathed a sigh of relief.

The man in the white flapping coat bobbed his head through the side door again. He nodded, and a smile glazed the corner of his mouth when he asked, "Who's next?" He looked directly at Vivian.

Vivian scanned the crowd and suggested the crying baby.

No one raised an eyebrow.

Vivian searched and found a clipboard she encouraged everyone to sign in according to his or her arrival time. The overhead bell dinged. A woman with triplets entered. She announced, "I called earlier and said I was running late!"

Vivian sighed and passed the clipboard to her and pulled what she could find of the waiting crowd's charts. Vivian asked, "Is anyone a new patient?" After seeing a few hands lift, she shuffled through the drawers and files, gathering the needed forms. She glanced at the owl wall clock and noticed its moving eyes indicating it was after four o'clock and the waiting room hadn't thinned much. She answered the phone and attached a brief note to each patient's file. Vivian was astonished with the lateness of Dr. Rose's practice. It was well into the evening, and her stomach threatened to growl.

"Hello, miss." The doctor swaggered to the desk, wearing a pleasant smile. "Thank you for jumping right in and coming to my aid. It's good to know the agency acted so quickly and sent me someone so qualified."

Vivian looked up and reached for the pencil behind her ear and tapped the counter. "Sorry to burst your bubble, Dr. Rose, but I'm not from any agency. My name is Vivian Litten, and I was summoned here at your request. I understand you needed documents of my mother's death, Carol Litten?"

He raked his smooth white hair and laughed. "You're not from the agency?"

"No." Vivian eyebrows arched, she asked, "Are you looking for a full-time receptionist?"

"I am, and you're hired. Now let's not waste any more of the day." He shrugged off his lab coat, hung it on a peg rail, and slipped on his tweed sports jacket. He ushered Vivian by the arm out the door. "I'm starved, aren't you?"

She shivered while adjusting her coat and juggling her purse and file. Her mouth parted, realizing how tired and hungry she became. Vivian didn't know anything about the doctor except he was older and looked fit. She removed his hand from her arm. "I drove myself to your office, and I'm perfectly capable of feeding myself."

"Well, Ms. Litten, let me introduce myself. My name is Dr. Keith Rose." A smile curved at the corners of his thin mouth. "I am pleased to meet you. Now, my dear, I'm over fifty years of age, and you are…well over," he arched brow, "let's say twenty-one, so don't be silly." He retrieved her arm and walked, stopping at the car parked at the curb. "Hop in! My driver will bring you back to the office after we eat." Raising a hand, he continued, "Or George will take you home and return your car later."

Vivian remained wide-eyed, staring up at the doctor. The chauffer opened the car door and bowed. The doctor, with a gentle nudge, encouraged her inside the vehicle, and the driver tipped his hat and closed the door. Vivian said, "I am hungry." She smoothed her skirt. "All right, Dr. Rose, dinner is fine."

She viewed the surroundings. Vivian could not believe she was sitting in a limousine. The doctor chuckled as he poured himself a glass of sparkling red wine and offered her an ice-cold bottle of water. After ten minutes of pure silence, they were in front of the town's mansion. Vivian gasped. She had passed by that mansion daily and had even looked through the tall black wrought-iron fence at the sight. She had always wondered who lived there. She willed calmness while staring at the dark ivy-covered brick mansion. She shivered as the car went through the opened gate. The driver parked on the cobblestone drive and turned off the engine. Her door opened, and the driver of the car, clicked his heels and bowed. The doctor reached for her elbow and walked her toward the mansion's front door where they were met by James, the butler.

"Hello, James."

Nodding, the butler said, "Dr. Rose, may I take your jacket and the lady's coat and purse?"

Vivian observed the butler's accent and took him to be German. He clicked his heels and swiveled walking down the hall. Vivian grabbed and shook the doctor's arm. "Where's he going with my coat, purse, and mother's file?"

4

The doctor patted her arm, never releasing the elbow, and replied, "James is only stepping into the library. Your purse, your coat, and your mother's file will be safe. James is a reliable man. He traveled with my father for years and stayed on as butler when my father purchased this residence." Dr. Rose's blue eyes gazed at Vivian's. "Now shall we eat?" The doctor's smile broadened.

Vivian blinked her eyes and squeaked, "Yes."

While they walked for what seemed like forever , Vivian viewed the portraits of men and women hanging on the walls.

The doctor said, "All forefathers and their wives." He guided her down another long hallway. Finally in front of her was a beautiful hand-carved cherry dining room table, twelve feet in length, laden with food. "Who's joining you, Dr. Rose?"

The doctor swung out his arm, offering Vivian a seat. "It will be only us eating here tonight." The doctor walked to the other end of the table and sat down.

She noticed the table could have easily seated eighteen.

"Miss, would you like ham or beef?" the servant in a chief's hat said.

"Beef please."

Another servant entered and asked, "Sweet potato or butter potatoes?"

She was about to answer when a soup was brought.

The server said, "Split pea or French onion, ma'am?"

Her eyes blinked and widened as she looked toward the doctor. He snapped his napkin in place and asked, "Does everything meet to your satisfaction?"

Vivian waited until the room cleared, then stood. She walked where the doctor was sitting and said, "Sir, it's hard having a conversation with you sitting so far away."

Keith scooted out his chair and laughter rumbled. "My dear, you are refreshing. Please allow me to sit across from you."

Vivian nodded.

He rang the bell, and a different servant came. Dr. Rose explained his desire to sit across from his guest, and the quiet change was made.

Vivian struggled to lift the oversize vase of flowers from her vision before sitting. She noticed the doctor appeared much older than she first thought, but even with age, he was attractive, very polite, and sweet. She felt welcome and safe. They talked about everything, and their time flew by. She yawned and apologized. "I'm sorry. My tummy is full, and my eyelids want to shut. Please take me to my car so you can have your evening back, what's left of it, and I, mine."

The doctor lifted from his chair and offered her his hand. She reached for his arm, and they began walking, and he said, "Since we need to examine the paperwork you brought concerning your mother, and might I add we need to discuss your employment, why don't you stay here tonight? Tomorrow I'm free after ten o'clock. We can chit-chat about matters then. Should you call or leave a message for anyone?"

Vivian gasped. "Dr. Rose! I don't know you!" She blushed.

He smiled and broke into a chuckle. Pausing, he said, "Vivian, I'm sure with my staff and the numerous bedrooms in this mansion, your well-being is quite safe."

"Sir, I am tired and would really appreciate a hot bath."

The doctor clapped his hands, and a woman-servant dressed in gray underneath a white apron appeared. She curtsied, her tiny hat secure on its place above her head, and said, "Ms. Litten, please follow me."

The winding staircase seemed to have a hundred steps. Vivian could hardly lift one foot in front of the other. She was pointed in the direction to the right and found a deep claw-foot tub filled with bubbles, and it carried a fresh citrus fragrance. There waited on a portable table a huge bath towel with washcloth and funny-shaped soaps. Also a handwoven basket held individual shampoos, cream rinses, and body oils. She noted the door hook held a new bathrobe, and on the floor were fuzzy slippers her size. Vivian turned to close the door, but the woman bowed, pulling the door close as she left the room.

Vivian soaked for a long while until she saw that her toes looked like an old prune. Being relaxed, she wanted to hop into bed. She stepped from the bathroom and didn't see anyone, and no one came. She was puzzled. Vivian couldn't find her clothes, and she didn't know where to sleep. Letting out a long sigh, she reasoned, "I'll go downstairs and look for the doctor. I hope he is still home." Retracing her steps, she was relieved seeing the hallway. Beginning down the corridor, she made a right and focused on the next hall. She saw books aligned on the wall unit and clasped her hands. She had found the library. Vivian searched her purse, making sure everything was still intact.

A deep voice came from the side corner, "Dear, what are you doing down here instead of being in bed?"

Vivian jump and her robe sagged. "I was looking for you, sir."

The doctor's blue eyes warmed and lifted, a smile replaced tired lines. "I'm yours."

Vivian groaned. "Well, that came out all wrong. Me and my big mouth! What I meant in saying was I don't know which bedroom I've been assigned, and I was hoping you would be here in the library reading or documenting or something." Vivian placed her hands on her hips and said sheepishly, "Would you please help me?"

His blue eyes squinted. "Why didn't you just pull the velvet rope by the bathroom door?"

She felt her neck heat and knew she was blushing. She looked at the floor and said, "I didn't know to pull the rope. I'm sorry."

He closed the gap between them and whispered, "You're such a child, a sweet loveable child. Come with me."

Before she could verbalize, he gathered her into his arms and ascended the stairs as if he was eighteen years old and she was a bag of air. He lowered her onto a massive bed of dark cherry wood, framed by four ceiling-to-floor posts. He lit the lamp by her bedside, and it cast overhead shadows through her netting, making the room speak of romance. When she dared breathe, she inhaled his manly scent and musk cologne, which lingered long after he left the room. She sunk into the downy feather mattress and whispered, "I think Dr. Keith Rose would make a gallant knight and shining armor." She quickly covered her mouth, for she saw his shadow. Vivian raised her head slightly, but it was heavy; her eyes blinked, and sleep took her.

The natural light streamed through the floor-to-ceiling window. Vivian stretched and rubbed her eyes. A smile lit across her face. Vivian leaped and padded into the bathroom. There her clothes were on a hanger, cleaned and pressed. The portable table now held a basket of little perfumes and makeup for the use. *Who could get used to this kind of living?* She dressed, noticing the time, and scurried to the library.

"Good morning, Vivian. Did you sleep well?"

She opened her mouth to answer, but a chef appeared and announced, "Breakfast is ready."

Again she was being escorted by the elbow by the doctor, who was in casual clothing. He led her outside where a metal-laced table sat in a stark but beautiful garden. The flowers were plentiful, and the massive ivy cascaded down the brick wall. In the center courtyard stood a three-tier fountain. It displayed therapeutic waters.

Dr Rose seated Vivian and slid her chair in. He sat across from her.

The chef asked if the eggs Benedict met her pleasure. Vivian watched him beam as she stated, "It's a wonderful breakfast."

The chef bowed as he backed away.

After breakfast, the doctor came behind Vivian. He said, "Let's go for a stroll in the gardens before we plunge into work." He patted her arm, and in silence, they wandered. Their gait slowed as they entered a parklike setting, where they again sat and enjoyed the bee balm, lilies, and the hanging baskets of marigolds. He frowned when he asked, "How old are you, Vivian?"

Vivian stuttered, "I'm…I'm…twenty-nine."

The doctor edged forward. "Do you have a beau?"

She squeaked, "Doctor, seriously, you mean like a boyfriend?"

He chuckled, then sobered. "Yes, I suppose that's what I'm asking."

Vivian squirmed and with an escalated voice, she replied, "Heavens no!" She adjusted her hair. "I've taken care of my mother before and after college." She became embarrassed and covered her face.

He remained calm. "Did you finish your education?"

Vivian cleared her throat, not looking up. "I did. I had selected a program for two years while finishing up high school." She glanced into his crinkled eyes and asked, "Why is education a requirement for employment with you?"

"My dear." He offered a hand and placed hers on his forearm, and again they walked. He continued, "No, working for me does not require any degree, but education is the window of tomorrow."

Vivian nodded. "Sir, may we go over my mother's file now?"

They strolled into the library and sat in the huge brown leather chairs. Vivian set near the edge because her feet could not touch the floor. The doctor eased back and relaxed one leg over the other. He shuffled through the file. He nodded his head a few times and said, "Well, everything is in order. I need to sign the form, and I will send it to the awaiting insurance company. You need not worry about a thing."

Vivian licked her lips and asked, "Did my mother leave any unsettled bills with you, sir?"

He tapped his knee and answered, "All has been settled."

Vivian let a breath. "Well, what about the job offer?"

With ease, the doctor spoke, "I'm open Monday through Friday from seven o'clock until closing. It's usually four o'clock when I'm with my last patient unless backed up. Are these hours acceptable for you?"

"What day do you want me to report on time?" Vivian toyed with her purse. "Is there a lunch break, and is there someone to do filing of the insurance forms?"

Tilting his head back, he answered, "If you need someone, hire them! The scheduling is yours to secure." Then pointing a finger, he said, "Oh, on Tuesday, from nine to twelve noon, I'm scheduled at the hospital for surgeries. Sometimes, there's a backlog. Office adjusting will be needed."

Vivian, with her file in hand and her notes from Dr. Rose stuffed them in her purse, smiled and stood. At the door, she slid into her coat. "I'll see you Monday morning bright and early."

The doctor walked near and touched Vivian's face. He bent and lightly brushed her lips.

She trembled and, with the back of her hand, wiped her mouth. "S-sir?"

He repeated his action, only slower this time, before stepping away. "Vivian, will you attend church with me tomorrow? My driver, George, will pick you up."

Feeling like a bubblehead, she walked out the front door. Her car was already parked in the driveway. She rolled down the window to thank the doctor for everything, but the good doctor was already standing by her car door.

He spoke, "Be ready by 8:15 a.m. We'll have breakfast first."

She half smiled and was glad when she heard the sound of the motor purr. Vivian shook her head. *Boy, I'm out of my league here.* She bit her lip, knowing Sunday morning with the doctor was a new beginning.

Vivian was dazed. She jerked upon hearing the cottage doorbell ding and was surprised by someone's constant knocking. She let out a held breath and saw David outside. He had arrived to decorate for Jathrow's party. Rushing to the door, she said, "For heaven's sake David, come on in."

David and Ty worked from early afternoon until time for the party. The western band finished tuning their instruments and began playing lively music.

Vivian, in her new colorful patio dress, red straw hat, and matching sandals, stepped in to the backyard. She saw all four male friends talking with ease, seemingly enjoying their time together. Vivian watched as Doreen made her appearance, arm in arm with a tall blonde-headed woman, who tapped Jathrow on the back.

Turning, Jathrow's smile widened, and dimples showed.

Vivian stared when Jathrow waltzed the blonde onto the dance floor. *He's a natural charmer.* The wilily woman was swaying back and forth way too close to a man she just met, especially one like Jathrow. She stood spellbound when the long-legged blond batted her eyes at Jathrow while he whirled her.

Doreen walked over to Vivian and said, "You better close your mouth, or you'll catch a fly." She smiled and nudged Vivian. "Don't you think they make an adorable couple?"

Vivian's full lips thinned, and her hands fisted. "I don't want to appear rude, but no! Not even a little." She stalked past Doreen and helped herself to a rack of ribs. Doreen edged her way again over to Vivian. "You did request single women to be at Jathrow's welcome home party, yes?"

Vivian kept stuffing her face. A few minutes later, Doreen left and greeted a medium-height sandy blonde. "Betty, glad you could make it. Let me introduce you to Jathrow," her voice carried.

Vivian caught a fleeting glance from Jathrow, and she threw rib bones at him. He laughed and turned sideways, facing Betty.

Vivian overheard Jathrow's cooing voice say, "Betty, I thank you for attending my welcome home party and for keeping me company."

Vivian wanted to walk away, but her feet wouldn't move. Her sparkling green eyes were daggered on to Jathrow.

He leaned in closely toward Betty, "What do you do for a living, Betty?"

Vivian somehow reached a lawn chair and eased herself down.

Doreen ushered Betty away from Jathrow and toward her husband, David.

After Jathrow loaded a plate, he lowered himself into a lawn chair next to Vivian with ease. Then Jathrow motioned for Betty.

Vivian stuck her tongue out at him.

Betty nodded to Jathrow and ended her talk with David. Betty all but leaped into Jathrow's lap. She wore short shorts, and her tank top was very revealing.

David called and waved for his wife, Doreen, to join him on the dance floor. Ty followed suit arm in arm with his wife, Lillian. The band music finally stopped, and the limbo was announced. As the music played, the bandleader called to Jathrow and Vivian to come out on the dance floor. The three single ladies went in front of Jathrow and David grabbed Vivian and placed her behind Jathrow. The three ladies screamed and swooned as they waited and watched Jathrow lean back and challenge the stick.

Vivian eyes threw darts at David, and with hands on her hips, she muttered, "Please." She went through the motions, giggling like everyone else. Ty's wife, Lillian stood behind Vivian and whispered, "Men always try to impress women. Just look at Ty limbo. Show off. You know he's a happily married man. Vivian, don't read so much into Jathrow's actions and by all means do not take it to heart."

Vivian arched her brows and cocked her head. "Lillian, what are you saying? There's nothing going on between Jathrow and me."

Lillian touched her shoulder and let the words trail, "You sure fooled me. I see how you can't keep your eyes off him, and he keeps watching you."

Vivian flung her hands to her mouth. "No, no, we are only friends. Like I am with your husband, Ty, and David, and Richard Sr. We've always been best friends."

Lillian's dark eyes rolled. She answered, "Please, I see all right. It's you who's not seeing clearly." She turned, waved, and yelled, "Ty, honey, here I am. Coming."

Vivian shook her natural red bob and breathed in slowly, scolding herself for her unwanted actions and being noticed. She scurried across the lawn and, from a distance, watched the limbo line.

The band cheered as Jathrow managed to win the backbreaking limbo. The three women stayed close around him. The band leader spoke into the mike and announced, "Gentleman, please select your favorite lady and swing her low and swing her high."

The lights dimmed.

5

The three single ladies flirted unmercifully with Jathrow, but with a wicked wink, he sashayed over to Vivian and snatched her hand. "Thanks for rescuing me," he said. Jathrow whirled her on the dance floor, and they moved to the music with ease. As the dance ended, he seductively dipped Vivian and breathed, "You're such a good sport."

She could only gasp.

"You look beautiful tonight. Nice dress!" His eyes of sea blue darkened.

Vivian locked eyes with Jathrow and lifted her right heel, planting it into the toe of his shoe. "A good sport, am I? Well!" She jerked free, her heart racing.

Jathrow's full lips thinned, and his blue eyes squinted; however, his grip tightened. Through gritted teeth, he spit, "I see you haven't danced in a while." He swung her around emphasizing each word, "Was your husband after all too old and neglectful?"

Vivian's hand flew through the air, striking his face. She froze at the hand imprint left on his cheek. Vivian broke loose and ran toward the cottage. She bolted the bedroom door and buried her face into a pillow. Her chest ached, and the tears flowed. She had trouble breathing.

Two hours later, the alarm clock buzzed. She sobbed even harder, causing dry heaves. Vivian gathered her knees under her chin. "I need to remember he sees me as a friend."

Her mind drifted. She was working for the famous Dr. Rose, enjoying her employment. She found it both rewarding, challenging, and demanding.

She would arrive in the office thirty minutes early to pencil in a daily lunch break. Sometimes the doctor would join her. Vivian was relaxed in his company and looked forward to their talks. She secretly admired his self-assurance and liked the way he made her feel safe.

The second month at work, the Keith arrived early, waving a gold-embossed invitation. "Vivian, read this please."

The invitation was addressed to him—it was a society ball.

"Will you grace me with your presence and attend the ball?" He leaned over the desk between patients and whispered, "I hate these black-tie affairs, but fund raisers are a must." The corner of his mouth lifted.

"Yes." Vivian reddened. "I'm flattered being asked to the society ball." But she knew he wanted to ward off other pursuing women. *Hmm, the doctor in his own rights is handsome and does carry himself well.*

It was the evening of the ball. Vivian paced the floor in her living room, waiting for Keith. He arrived in a black long-tail tuxedo, which molded his lean body. The porch light emphasized his silvering hair. If she hadn't caught him fidgeting with the shirt collar, she would have disagreed that he didn't like gala events.

Vivian spent her entire week's salary on an evening dress and shoes for the event. She enjoyed the warming darts from his soft blue eyes. Yet at the ball, the ladies, married or single, beckoned him on the dance floor.

Drinking a bottled water, she thought, *This evening marks four months since Keith and I first met. It seems like I've known him my entire life. And finally we're on first-name basis.*

Keith called the next Saturday afternoon, inviting her to a formal dinner and theater date. She agreed and was amazed how smooth their evening passed. The night air felt crisp but refreshing. When his driver pulled up in front of her house, she was dumbfounded when Keith sent him away. Vivian questioned, "Where's he going?"

But his hand clasped over hers, reaching for her house key. He shoved the front door open and closed it with gentleness.

Vivian licked her lips and asked, "Would you like a cup of coffee or something?"

He nodded, making himself at home, sitting on the sofa. He picked up her photo album and glossed through it. Vivian entered the room and extended a hot cup of liquid to him as she balanced an iced bottle water for herself. He took both the cup offered and the water, placing them on the coffee table. He reached for her hands and tugged Vivian onto his lap and touched her cheek.

She trembled.

He said, "I'm not getting any younger, dear, and I believe you've become comfortable around me and know my ways." He paused kissing her lightly. "I've decided we should marry! You're such a child in so many ways, but adorable." He moved her to the sofa and unfolded himself. His blue eyes searched hers. "Vivian, you are smart, good-looking, and a trustworthy woman. I even understand you most of the time." He watched her eyes widened, and his hands framed her beet-red face.

"Keith—um, Dr. Rose, I trust I haven't misled you in any way. I'm not trying to hone in on your bachelorhood." Seconds passed. "I do however enjoy our time together, and I feel safe with you. You're such a gentleman!" Vivian straightened a strand of mischievous hair, placing it behind her ear. "You intrigue me with your work, wisdom, and worldly ways."

He remained silent, and time ticktocked away. Vivian walked into the kitchen, carrying his cup and her now warm bottled water. "Keith, I know you care deeply for your patients. You're kind, gentle, and loyal. It's strange, but it's your caring ways that drew me to you. But would that ever be enough?" She shook her head.

He strolled to her side, taking her hands in his, and slid down on one knee. He gazed upward. "Vivian, I'm old enough to be your father, but I value you and will give you anything you want. There will be no prenuptial for you to sign. It's all yours if you will care for me in my retirement age until death." He squeezed her hands and continued, "You're dependable and trustworthy, and you have wooed me. Say yes to being my wife." His thin bottom lip quivered. "Vivian, in my own subtle way, I do love you, and marriage makes perfect sense." He held his head higher and stood. He said, "I do have one request."

Vivian shifted from one foot to another, lowering her head, "What would your request be, Doctor?"

Bending down, he whispered in her ear, "You bear me one child. Boy or girl, it doesn't matter. I want us to be a family." He chuckled, throwing his head backward. "I never thought of myself begging, nor did I think of myself wanting marriage, but, my precious dear, this I want only with you. Now will you say yes?"

Before a word could be uttered, he reached into his pocket.

Keith produced and opened a black velvet box, which held a magnificent-sized pear-shaped diamond.

Vivian's eyes went moist as a tear trickled down. She bit her bottom lip and moved away. Thoughts of Jathrow flooded her mind. *If only he had came back for me or called to state any desire for me.* She twisted her hands. Her heart pounded faster, and her lips quivered. She answered, "How could I ever say no to you."

He smiled broadened as he twisted the fitted ring on her third finger on her left hand. He bent and kissed her. "Dear, may we hurry this wedding? I've wasted years. Can you pull this together in a month?"

Admiring her ring, she said, "Doctor, are you kidding? It will take months of planning!

Keith began to pace. "I don't want to wait. Oh, Vivian." He turned and placed a hand on her shoulder. "I want you in my life and in my bed!" He moved closer. With smiling blue eyes, he asked, "So when?"

Vivian felt redness rise from her neck up to her face. She cleared her throat. "We can say our wedding vows in three months? You'll need to deal with the press. I will make myself available as needed."

He broke into laughter, then asked, "Want me to call the minister?"

Vivian held up her hands. "Keith, you'll need to do everything for me. All the planning only. Don't select my wedding dress."

"Darling, I'll supply you with contact names and numbers. You can choose your own wedding attendant." He frowned. "Vivian, listen to me." He took her hands in his. "You'll need my friends and acquaintances someday. And, darling, so you know, I believe in your writing skills. You should explore your options, and mark my word, you will be known worldwide as an author."

Days, weeks, months passed, and finally the wedding arrangements were accomplished. Keith had the mansion's ballroom opened for their special day. David escorted certain invited guests to the oversized conference room. Ty and Richard Sr. catered their refreshments. Dr. Rose socialized with them for an hour and answered their questions and the press.

Vivian, in passing the conference room, noticed her male friends. A giggle slipped from her. She adored and admired their serving attitude and liked the tuxedos they were wearing. She hurried on to her dressing room and forty-five minutes later she peered from the curtain and watched guests being seated in the beautiful ballroom. It was decorated in all shades of soft pink fabric and fancy tooling. It took her breath away.

The soft music began to play, the minister stepped into position, and Keith followed. Then he stood in front of the altar, facing the crowd. Soon David, Ty, and Richard Sr., who were like the Three Musketeers, stood on Keith's side.

Vivian bit her bottom lip and momentarily glanced over the seated guests, searching for the one familiar face. But hope died—he was not there. With an audible sigh, she said, "Who are these people?" Vivian became sweaty and cold. *Is getting married what I want?* Panic rose. She whispered, "I need a moment for me!"

Her female wedding planner, Tammy, helped her exit through the side door. Vivian stood among the mansion's garden. She breathed in a long breath then held a hand to her chest. Keith had thought of everything. There were roses, daisies, and lavender herbs planted. The beds were glorious. She smelled the blooming roses and shook her head when the sound of water splashing caught her attention. Vivian spotted two-dozen or more white swans playing. Vivian pinched herself, warning herself not to cry.

The flutes sounded, and Tammy stood, tapping her foot by the side door. Vivian scurried inside. The harpist strummed, and Vivian, once again on tiptoe, glanced over the crowd. She bit her bottom lip. No Jathrow.

I sent him a personal note inside the wedding invitation. Why hadn't he bothered to RSVP?

Even her three male friends, who were her school buddies, quit mentioning Jathrow's name after the doctor made the formal engagement announcement.

Vivian saw Keith. He was fingering his shirt collar. Vivian willed down her jumpy emotions and in silence thought, *Keith is a golden treasure for any woman. And a solid good man.* She straightened her lacy sweetheart, fit and flare ivory gown and fluffed her unmanageable red curls.

The diamond tiara was in place. Tammy draped the sheer flowing veil on Vivian's head.

The select organ music began, and the bride's maids, her friends' wives, one by one walked the aisle.

Vivian exhaled when the music shifted. The doctor's old friend, Walter Price, appeared at her room and bowed. He offered her his arm. The trumpets blew, echoing through the mansion, and then the traditional wedding march began. Organ notes held.

Vivian took in quick breaths, stepped outside her dressing room, and wide-eyed locked eyes with Keith's. She saw tenderness in his blue eyes.

As they stood before the minister, he mentioned the doctor's pledge of love toward Vivian and then the minister spoke of her pledge on faithfulness to the doctor, before continuing with the two exchanging vows, but when the minister said, "I pronounce you man and wife," she went numb and weak. The minister waved his hand and, with a huge smile, finished, "Dr. Keith Rose, you may kiss your blushing bride."

Vivian felt Keith's breath. She tasted his familiar cold thin lips on hers.

Vivian thought, *If only his lips could be warm like the light in his eyes.*

Fate had sealed their forever promise. The crowd howled, "They're married!"

Keith held her arm and walked with her to the reception area, beaming. The photographer was waiting. The bulb flashed. It seemed like hours later that Keith graced her hand and led her onto the dance floor. Vivian adjusted her shoulders to relax and gave herself a pep talk. *Come on now. You've danced with the doctor many times.* She took her position and tilted her head. *Husband and wife.* She plastered on a smile and squeezed his hand.

The night to come was in slow motion. The doctor enjoyed the removing of her garter and the cheering from the people.

She toyed with her ring and answered the pleas of the bride's bouquet tossing. The crowd clapped and became louder as the newly trained receptionist caught Vivian's arrangement.

The trumpets sounded again, and Vivian was whisked away to the awaiting decorated car. She saw the Just Married sign and the trailing tin cans. The driver smiled, bowed, and opened the car door. Vivian took a step. From the corner of her eye, she thought she saw Jathrow and gasped. Keith eyes followed hers. She blinked and looked again, but the sidewalk and street were empty. The doctor squeezed her hand and said, "Let's go, my love."

Vivian slid across the seat and smoothed her dress. She felt Keith's piercing blue eyes search hers. Without a smile, he cupped her chin, angled his body, and lowered his lips, claiming hers. Moving his firm hand to her shoulder, he said, "Jathrow Mowey had his chance. It's time to forget him. You're mine as said before God until death do us part. You promised."

Vivian trembled and through choked words said, "Keith, you're everything any woman would ever want." A single tear slid down her cheek. "I'll always honor you and stay by your side. I'm thankful for my marriage and to such a wonderful person as you, Dr. Rose." Vivian warmly patted his hand and regained her smile. They looked from the rear window and waved as George drove away. The people faded from sight. She knew destiny was at hand, and soon her promise to the doctor would be kept in being his wife in every way.

A series of quick knocks sounded on her bolted bedroom door. Vivian jerked. "Who's there?"

David said, "Your friend."

She opened the door ajar. Then David's foot entered. He said, "Everyone is gone from Jathrow's welcome home party. I told them you had a migraine." He offered her his handkerchief.

She reached for it and dabbed around her eyes. "Oh, David, thanks for caring and helping me out." He left her alone.

Moments later, she walked in the living room. David nodded, then began loading the vases into the truck, where Ty was waiting for him. Vivian walked to the porch and waved until the taillights disappeared.

Suddenly, a warm hand touched her back. Her breath caught. It was Jathrow. She turned, and his warm full lips were within contact, but pride roared. Vivian stepped aside, crossed her arms, and emphasized, "Excuse me!"

He dropped his hand and let her pass, "Viv, wait."

That evening on the porch Jathrow had said, "I need a woman to attend the attorney's fundraiser with me who will not expect any friendly favors at the end of the night. Help me out Viv and go with me?" He winked.

She couldn't refuse her friend in need.

Socialites from different states and a few countries were in attendance at the fundraiser.

Vivian was still in awe at how Jathrow had hoodwinked her into attending the event with him. She wanted to stay angry with him. But in all fairness, Jathrow had sent flowers and apologized for his rude statement about her husband, Keith.

A hostess motioned to Jathrow. He clutched Vivian's arm. He shifted and dodged most people. At the table, they greeted the people . A seven-course meal was served as the jazz band played softly.

An hour later, a young woman stepped to the mic and called out for Jathrow.

Jathrow's warm lips brushed Vivian's cheek. On the platform, his crooner voice carried through the air, captivating the guests. He said, "Ladies and gentlemen, dig deep in your pocket for the event you've been waiting for, the auction. It's now!"

The woman announcer from her area held up a contemporary art oil painting, by an American artist, David Heath. "Now how much am I offered?"

Jathrow raised his checkbook and said, "I'll bid three thousand dollars."

Vivian gasped.

The announcer then said, "Going, going, gone." And kissed Jathrow.

His dimples deepened. Jathrow walked the room, working it, beckoning others to bid.

Photographers snapped picture after picture. Jathrow posed easily with the socialites, women models, and married or single women alike. No matter their age, they flocked around him, showing their availability.

The bandleader motioned to Jathrow. He walked to their area and announced, "It's time for the first waltz of the evening."

Jathrow came over to Vivian and reached for her hand. He glided with her on the dance floor. No one else existed between them until there was an interruption.

A toothpick-framed female tapped Jathrow on the shoulder. A new song had begun. Jathrow winked and dropped arms with Vivian. He scrunched his eyes and bowed to the nervy woman. Vivian watched as he swayed with the music and laughed. Mixed emotions tumbled through her. She thought Jathrow could have turned down the other woman. Vivian became lightheaded and sweaty. She saw her late husband's friend by the punch table, and she edged her way there. "Walter, are you with a date?"

He grinned and nodded in the other direction. "Vivian, my dear, the date in which graced my arm, has appeared to hook up with the man of the hour, Jathrow." Chuckling, he began walking toward the front door. In turn, Walter said, "I'm too old for all this...fanfare. I gave my pledge to the fund raiser." He eyed Vivian before continuing, "I was just leaving."

Vivian touched his arm. "Would you mind dropping me off at the cottage?"

His forehead wrinkled when he asked, "Do you mind riding in a jeep?"

6

"You're kidding, right, Wayne?"

"No. I wanted a jeep while I was in medical school, but was too poor." He motioned her to follow.

At the jeep, Vivian tried stepping inside, but wearing six-inch heels, she needed Walter's help. The back roads were dark, and the way was bumpy. Walter came to an abrupt stop. Vivian didn't wait. Her dress caught in the door, but she closed her eyes and jumped. On the ground, she blew Walter a farewell kiss.

He nodded and waited until she disappeared inside the cottage.

Vivian slipped from her torn gown and placed it in the closet with her matching shoes and purse. She removed her streaked makeup and wiggled into her old tattered shorts and splotchy tank top. Vivian felt a story coming to mind. She powered up the computer and began to type. Hours passed. The fiction was alive, vivid, and good. The mystery plot deepened. Just then, the house phone rang, causing her to jump. She giggled. "Hello. This is Vivian. How may I help you?"

She heard rushed breaths and recognized it was Jathrow. He said, "I won't be in tonight. There's um…some unfinished business to take care of. I just didn't want you worrying or waiting up."

Vivian was surprised, numb, and speechless listening. Before disconnecting, she detected a woman's giggle. Vivian willed down her rising temper. *He never came back for me after college, and he didn't answer the note placed in my wedding invitation. You think time would heal all wounds?* The tears fell as she plunked away on the computer keys. She whispered, "I even asked him if he had any romantic feelings toward me, so what was I thinking?" She bowed her head on her arms, "Jathrow will never change. Once a playboy, always a playboy. It meant nothing to him that I kissed him. He pushed you away, fool."

Vivian reached for her cell phone, and at that moment, she dialed her agent, Samuel Gee. On the fifth ring, he answered. "Samuel, this is Vivian."

With sleepiness in his voice, "Do you know what time it is?"

Her voice cracked. She snapped, "Yes! It's morning, and Mr. Gee it's time to start earning your money. Call and schedule my appearances and book signings. I intend to be on the first flight out of here."

She grabbed her luggage and slammed her clothing in it, then placed a long-distance call to her daughter.

Jacey answered, "Mom, what's going on?"

Vivian sighed. "I'm leaving for my tour, and I'll be in Australia soon." "When?"

Jamming the last suitcase closed, she said, "I'm waiting on a cab now. Mr. Gee has been pressuring me on these appearances and book signings for weeks, and you know the public doesn't wait. Oh, I hear the horn. See you soon."

Vivian set her suitcases out for the cabbie to load while she placed a sticky note on the coffee machine addressing Jathrow.

> When you leave, lock up. Place the cottage key in the yellow flowerpot on the edge of the porch. Thanks for contacting me about a rental room. Jathrow, if you're ever in town again and need a place to stay, the whole cottage may be rentable. It was interesting seeing you again. I'm promoting my new novel, The Key. You know duty calls.
>
> Signed, Vivian

Jathrow parked the loaner car in the driveway. The dawn was breaking. He yawned and stretched his legs and noticed the cottage appeared dark and empty. Scratching his head, he unlocked the front door and moseyed to the coffee machine. It was still warm, and attached was a sticky note addressed to him. Jathrow's stomach knotted after reading the note. His confidence became shaken.

Vivian had always been there for him and had supported him in all his dreams and decisions. Even when he left Richmond, Virginia, in his youth to chase a career. She had traveled with their friends when he graduated from law school, along with David, Ty, and Richard Sr., and they shared a great evening celebrating with dinner and reminiscing.

Jathrow poured the hot liquid and took a sip. Vivian had never cornered him about why he hadn't come home those many years ago. He took another sip. He hadn't heard from Vivian again until her first short story was released. She called, and they talked for hours about nothing and yet everything. Then he received a signed copy of Vivian's first book.

Jathrow tapped the counter. The next time he heard from Vivian was in the shocking wedding invitation. Enclosed was an engagement picture of her and the great Dr. Rose, with a personal note asking him if he had any romantic feelings toward her, and then there in great boldness was a request to RSVP if he would come to the wedding.

Jathrow rubbed his chin and admitted to himself, *I came back to Virginia because Vivian was getting married. Without* RSVP.

He had wanted to speak and spend time with Vivian, but the big day approached, and he chickened out. Unknowingly to anyone, and like a coward, he watched from a distance Vivian and Dr. Keith Rose pledge their undying vows. An unsettled sadness engulfed his heart and lungs. He was weak, and his breathing became shallow when the words "I do" were said. Then he realized, what would he have said to Vivian? So he fled and had somehow escaped the house and ran to the corner. Just outside the drugstore, he observed Vivian sliding into the marked vehicle. The Just Married sign seemed huge. Jathrow backed into the store, clinging to his chest. He was sure it would explode. He was raging with mixed emotions.

Jathrow stared out the kitchen window and was still puzzled. He took another sip of cold coffee and raked his hair into a ponytail. He looked upward and said, "Why do I feel such a loss, an emptiness." The complexity settled deep within. He tipped the cup and set it down. Closing the blinds, he walked into the bathroom, turned on the shower, and promised to wash this entire dredge away.

After towel-drying, Jathrow slipped on his shorts and laid down. He placed a hand behind his head, letting his mind again journey to the fundraiser auction night. Lots of women were present and one very persistent assistant event planner ploying for his attention. Oh, and then there was Betty!

Grabbing a pillow, he jabbed it. His headache had eased, but his mind wouldn't rest. Vivian did clap at his speech when encouraging the selective group of people to freely open up their wallets and bid at the auction fundraiser. They seemed to have fun together, talking, eating, and dancing, until he caught a glimpse of Vivian's departure. She left with an older man, and his stomach clenched in knots.

Jathrow rolled out of bed, raking his matted long hair and raving, *Didn't I let Vivian know that I was the main drawing card for the auction? I'm sure I explained.* He walked through the house. *After all I was the attorney elected to entice people to spend their monies.* Glancing around, he saw the clip article, on the fundraiser, on the top of Vivian's scrapbook.

Jathrow shoved into his jeans while thoughts lingered on him. He was manly, arrogant, and vain. He even laughed when people guessed his age in the midthirties instead of midfifties. He worked out religiously to stay fit, and he was wise to become well-educated. Even his confidence rose when his prestige title came to power.

Jathrow shuddered as he recalled how life was before graduation from high school. He discovered that the man with his mother in the picture was not his father. His mother took ill and died suddenly. Richmond, Virginia, had nothing to offer him. Leaving the state was in his best interest the same night of his graduation.

He had arrived in the big city LA where Jathrow met Stella Ball in the airport bar. Stella was an older handsome woman and appeared highly educated. He was seventeen and lied about his age and showed false ID.

It was a place I never should have entered, but my sin looked good. Stella Ball displayed an outward adornment calling him a boy toy. She willfully paid for the drinks, and had invested her time with only him. When the close of the evening came, Stella Ball invited him to her place for lodging. While he stayed there, she taught a willing student how to become a man. Jathrow enjoyed his newfound ways of pleasuring women with words and affection. He guarded his heart as he strutted comfortably in his own skin. He had conquered manhood and worldly habits, but a college education was missing. However, Jathrow stayed on with Stella for two years, where he skimped and pinched his pennies.

Sleep evaded him. Jathrow slammed the pillow to the headboard and finally flung his legs over the edge of the bed. He decided to sit at the computer and fill out the necessary fundraiser report. Then he sent it to his business partner, Stan Trout, on the e-mail.

Jathrow stretched his legs and glanced at the computer and was relief seeing the arrows proceeding. He glanced at the note from Vivian. "Why hadn't she mentioned a book appearance / signing tour?" He hunched his shoulders. "I guess it was none of my business."

He decided called his buddy Richard Sr.

"Hello this is Richard Pair Sr."

Jathrow laughed and said, "I know who you are. Say, would you like to rowdy up the guys and go fishing? Like old times."

Richard Sr. cleared his throat. "Jathrow, some of us have to work for a living." Then he laughed. "I'll give them a call. Hold on. I'll try conferencing us."

Ty answered, "Ty's Cleaning Services."

Richard Sr. stated, "Wait, Ty." A short beep sounded when Richard Sr. said, "David, wait." Another long beep sounded then Richard Sr. said, "All right men, Jathrow Mowey is on the line with us. He asked if we would like to go fishing today. Well, what say ye?"

"I'm free," Ty aired. "I scheduled today off after the black-tie event."

David said, "Count me in. Is Vivian coming? Jathrow, you two seemed like real connections were made last night, especially on the dance floor."

Jathrow interrupted, "No way! Vivian left. She's on tour with her book. Come on now. I'm sure she informed you, men."

"Hey, hey," Richard Sr. belted. "Testy, testy, ease up, Jathrow. I knew there had been talk about a tour, but I didn't know the tour had been confirmed."

Ty said, "It's news to me."

David hollered, "Me too."

Jathrow hit the table. "What? Viv left me a note instructing me where to leave the cottage key when I leave. She indicated I could rent the whole cottage out next year. I think Vivian is angry with me. Women."

Richard Sr. gave a low whistle, and the other men sighed.

Jathrow asked, "Well, are we going fishing or not? Ty, do you need any help with the boat?"

In unison, Jathrow heard, "Meet you at the cottage in an hour." The lines clicked. Silence.

❧❦❧

Jumping from his work truck, David said, "I brought food and drinks." He held up an odd container. "And the bait."

Ty stood beaming beside his old station wagon, which pulled his boat. He yelled, "Jathrow, help David. Grab the fishing poles and bait. Bring them on the boat."

Richard Sr. came carrying the tackle box.

The four friends found themselves humming "Old McDonald."

David checked the boat and made adjustments and took his place along with Jathrow and Richard Sr., leaving Ty to slide in behind the station wagon wheel and drive.

The men were headed toward Long Bay Point. They passed the hustle-bustle area where people lived with ease in their houseboats. They saw every shape and size of houseboats resting semisecluded among the peninsula of trees.

When the men neared the coastal shore, Jathrow said, "Isn't the water blue and clear as it was when we were boys? Remember how we enjoyed the privacy of the trees and the white sandy beach?"

The men glanced at each other and sang, "Memories."

Ty backed the boat to the lake, and the men pushed it off from shore. David adjusted the bobber and was first in casting out a fishing line. It wasn't long until there was a nibble. The bobber went under, pulling the fishing line on a ramped run. David stood, and pulled back, reeling in the line. The men cheered him on. The fish was caught. David exaggerated on the size of his catch. The men looked at one another and laughed, which led to them holding their sides.

Ty edged away from the men to the other side of the boat and claimed his fishing spot. He placed his faithful red fishing cap on his head, cast out his line, sat down, and waited for the big moment. Richard Sr. had joined David, which was in his marked north position, when Jathrow appeared in the water in hip boots. He used a fly rod. After several casting, Jathrow's fishing was successful.

The men spent hours baiting and hooking fish, but freedom was given to their day's catch. The men's eyes dropped to the glistening sand as Jathrow from the boat shimmied from his clothes, shucking down to his briefs. He jumped into the water and challenged, " Get in the water!"

Treading, Jathrow felt years roll back in time, except a dull ache lulled in his chest. Pushing aside his personal feelings, he teased the men, and they bantered back.

They all swam to the private beach area where the No Swimmers warning sign was still posted. Just like in their youth.

David protected the sandwiches and managed the water jug. The men high-fived and waited like birds to be fed. They lounged around, enjoying the day, relaxing, and exchanged boyhood tales.

Richard Sr. glanced Jathrow's way. "Have you ever thought about moving back to Virginia?"

Jathrow rubbed his chin. "I've been considering that move. I would like to bring my law practice here, but…"

Ty and David chuckled.

Ty teased, "Yeah, no beach babes."

David said, "There's not much happening in this part of the state especially after five o'clock in the evening. You blink, and you've missed the said action." David paused while packing up the leftovers, "Jathrow, seriously, there's not one noncommittal single woman living here. They all want marriage, children, and the white picket fence." David shrugged his shoulders.

Ty mumbled, "I don't know why anyone wouldn't want the total package. Just look at me."

Jathrow ruffled Ty's straight black hair and said, "Yes, we are looking at you and the few extra pounds you're carrying. We all know you're a happily married man."

Jathrow brows narrowed. He pointed a finger at each man and said, "That goes for each of you. I know you're happy contented homebodies."

"Jathrow, how have you managed to escape our happy marriage of blissfulness all these years? We've seen the magazines and read the newspapers. They keep us well informed about you. And we were exposed of your talented ways at the auction dundraiser." David's brows rose.

Jathrow kicked at the sand. "Ah, men, most of what I do anymore is just for show. It's expected of me or, say, my image." Jathrow raked his hands through his blond hair and continued, "I asked Vivian to attend the fundraiser with me. So I wouldn't to be stuck with bimbos. Being a friend, Vivian agreed to be my date. However, last night became a hot mess!" He waited then said, "Vivian left with an old fellow, and I ended up stuck with Nurse Betty. Betty had worked a double shift at the hospital and was sleep deprived. She had indulged in a glass of wine before attending the fundraiser. Nurse Betty drank throughout the night with lack of food or coffee. Suddenly the evening took a toll on her. I couldn't leave Nurse Betty stranded. I also didn't want any wrong gossip. "It took a lot of black coffee and a listening ear before she was stable enough to leave in a cab by herself. I was sure glad the twenty-four-hour diner on the outskirts of town was open."

In his gruff voice, Richard Sr. said, "You used Vivian again!" He stood and faced Jathrow and threw a right punch.

Jathrow immediately jumped to his feet, raising his fist.

David blocked his arm.

Ty stepped in front of Richard Sr. just after he glazed Jathrow's cheek again. Ty wrestled with Richard Sr. and hauled him to the ground.

David held Jathrow's shoulders and yelled, "Guys, simmer down. We all care about Vivian."

The men eased their hands down by their sides.

David began pacing. Through gritted teeth, David directed a question to Jathrow, "Do you know Vivian only married the doctor because you never encouraged a relationship with her? Why didn't you come back for her years ago?"

Jathrow held his chin and said, "We've always been friends. Good friends." He gasped, "Are you indicating Vivian felt womanly for me?"

Richard Sr. reached for Ty's hand and bounced back on his feet. He stepped forward and with fisted hands, thundered, "Jathrow, for someone who's so wise and worldly knowledgeable about women, you sure are dumb!" Richard Sr.'s face went beet red. He kicked the warm white sand. "Vivian has always been sweet on you! I know. Before my missus., in Ty's younger days and mine, we asked her out on dates. But Vivian turned us down."

Ty nodded.

"She clarified that unless we were all in a group, she would not go anywhere with us. Vivian made sure we understood we were only good friends. She once said, 'I would go out with Jathrow if he asked.'"

Jathrow paled. He stumbled and sat down. He whispered weakly, "I...I didn't know she was interested in me. Even when she wrote and spoke of romance, I thought she was joking." He cleared his throat. "Could someone like Vivian ever notice me? Really?" He glanced at his three friends, wide eyed. "Are you sure?"

Ty nodded.

David placed a heavy hand on Jathrow's shoulder. "I'm sorry to jar you back to reality, but look at the water!"

"What angry waves. We better go, men." Jathrow shook his head.

The air changed.

7

The winds whipped up the sand, and the sky blackened. It threatened an old-fashioned downpour. The men waded into the water and swam toward the boat.

However, with each stoke they made, great effort was a struggle against the waves and the current.

Jathrow made his way to the boat first and hooked a leg over the side. He flung his hair and, balancing on the side, held out a hand for Richard Sr. "Friend, the raging water even took a toll on me and I surf!"

Richard Sr. was puffing.

No one spoke for moments. The rains streamed, and the lightning struck. Abruptly the thunder cracked through the air. Ty motioned Richard Sr. to lift the anchor. David offered his hands, and together they edged the anchor in. Jathrow jumped into the water to shove off. Both David and Richard Sr. reached out and grabbed Jathrow to safety. The men scrambled into their clothes.

Whirling winds and crashing waves grew larger. The boat's engine refused to crank. The men rotated turns and struggled as they rowed. The north shoreline wasn't far, but the men fought a continuous tug of war.

When David stepped on land, he let out a sigh of relief. Jathrow worked with the men to secure the boat back on to Ty's station wagon. Traveling in the old station wagon with a swerving boat seemed to take longer than their beginning journey.

Back at the cottage, Jathrow said, "Thanks men for today. We'll remember this outing for a long time. It was fun and eye-opening. Let's get together again real soon."

The men laughed while shaking their heads.

Still in the huddle, Richard Sr. said, "Jathrow, think about settling here." He walked a little closer and placed a hand on Jathrow's shoulder. "Call me anytime." The clouds rolled swiftly, and the sky darkened more with shades of purple. Patches of lightning flashed again, the wind howled, and the large raindrops fell quick.

David hopped in his truck, waved, and barreled down the gravel road; Ty in his station wagon chugged close behind with the boat rocking on its carrier.

Richard Sr. in his Cadillac was behind Ty but with a safe distance between them.

Jathrow ran inside the cottage and took a chance against the lighting and showered, zipped his jeans, and towel-dried his long hair. His stomach growled, so he warmed the leftover soup and fixed a cheese sandwich. After placing the dishes in the sink, he walked to the covered porch, carrying a mug of hot steaming coffee.

The weather was fierce. Jathrow sat himself into a rocker. He propped up his feet and watched the storm. Lightning filled the sky, carrying its own magnificent show of thunder and its orchestrated sounds of snaps and irregular crackles. The earth shook, the winds whipped more, and the rain turned into fifty-cent hail. Jathrow once again was forced inside. The electric flickered, and the lights went out. He felt his way in search of matches and candles. Jathrow shivered as thoughts of Vivian invaded his mind, and an unexpected loneliness hounded him for the second time that day. Jathrow decided it was time for him to leave Virginia a week early and head back to LA. He flipped the lid on his cell and made the call.

As quick as the storm came in, it left. Within an hour, a honking noise sounded, and Jathrow loaded his luggage in the trunk of the cab. He motioned for the cabbie to wait. Once again inside the cottage, he placed a written card by the unplugged coffee maker for Vivian. He backed out the door, locked it, and stored the key in the yellow pot. When the cabbie pulled away, he noticed how the old fence would need another coat of paint and the climbing roses would need again to be pruned. From the corner of his eye, he saw sacks of mixed flower seeds right where Vivian left them. Jathrow vowed to call Richard Sr. and have him check on their friend's place while she was away.

The Virginia airport seemed small in comparison to LA, but it was efficient. Jathrow checked in his luggage, leaving him with a carry-on tote. Walking through the gate, the overhead speaker made an eerie noise. The steward announced flight 233 was ready for take off. He glanced at his ticket and made a mad dash.

Jathrow was accustomed to first class; however on this plane, the seating was all the same. He was wedged in a narrow row and a slender seat. When the person next to him squeezed in the row, a good portion of his seat was used. Jathrow leaned back, closed his eyes, and muttered under his breath, "I have four hours and thirty-four minutes until I land."

The huge LA airport was a welcoming sight. Jathrow adjusted his silk tie and slipped on his jacket. He gathered his luggage and stopped for the luxury of having his shoes shined. He tossed the young lad a big tip and whistled, waving a cab. He was waiting for the happiness he usual felt when he's back in the bustle of the big city.

He entered his condo and saw the nagging blinking green light on his landline phone. He was glad he hadn't used his cell phone while he was away to check on his messages. He had wanted solitude and serenity from his hectic daily schedule and wanted to be refreshed. However, he was back. Jathrow glazed out the high-rise condo and asked, "Is this what I want to come home to?"

He loosened his tie, took off his jacket, and rolled his shirt cuffs under. With a pad and pencil in hand, he hit the nonstop blinking button. Ms. Bella, in her high-pitched, sweet voice, had called five times, asking where he had vanished. He paused the button and gave her a second thought. *Hmm, she's tall, sophisticated, and the councilor's sister. A blonde and a size 2.* He chuckled as he made comparison of her to Vivian. Ms. Bella was not healthy-looking in any way. Jathrow raised his brows. "Where did that thought come from?" He shook his head and pushed the button again to listen.

Jathrow heard Stan Trout's rushed words about a client's urgent request. Jathrow shook his head, for Mr. John Glitching was one of the company's most valuable clients. Mr. John Glitching's billionaire son, Tom Glitching, flew into town and caused a big ruckus. Mr. Trout said, "Their client expected the firm to handle all reckless and damage done claimed by the Main Strip Hotel. Mr. John Glitching wanted the firm to use quality control with the women his son showed around town."

Jathrow heard strangeness in Stan's voice. He immediately opened his cell phone and called his business partner, Stan.

At first ring, Jathrow heard, "It's about time you called!"

"What's the latest on billionaire Tom's adventures?"

"Can you hear me?" Stan belt out.

"Yes. Stan?"

"Jathrow, you don't know the half of it. I have Tom at my place, and he fell asleep. This is my fourth day baby-sitting him. I hope he sobers up soon. Jathrow, I placed a call in at the hotel. The owner will work with our firm and has promised no news leaks. You needed to settle things and square Mr. Tom Glitching's image. Here's the hotel's address."

Jathrow heard hesitation in Stan's voice.

"Here is the address of the women believed to be with Tom. Work your charm. Don't let any information, pictures, or given story leak out to the press. Oh, Tom is waking up. We're taking a drive and discuss this situation. I hope with Daddy's hefty check, penned with lots of zeros, Tom Glitching will invest it in an unheard private island and vanish."

"I understand. I'll call when this ordeal is finished." Jathrow took a needed shower before riveting his red convertible BMW toward the hotel.

A man was pacing outside the building. He signaled Jathrow and ushered them into a private office. There, the beady-eyed man introduced himself. "I'm Mr. Seasons." With a hand out, he asked, "And you are… Attorney Mowey?"

Jathrow nodded and clasped Mr. Season's hand.

Mr. Seasons said, "Let me show you the suite's damages. It's extensive. Mr. Trout assured me the repairs will not be an issue."

In the room, the estimate was handed to Jathrow. He briefly glanced at the damages and placed a hand on his hip. "Mr. Seasons, this suite will be better than new." Jathrow stepped backward, never losing eye contact and pulled out the company checkbook. "Thank you, Mr. Seasons, for handling this matter discreetly. This should cover the remodeling, and here's something extra for your inconvenience. Please sign this release form." Both shook hands, and Jathrow placed the signed form back into the briefcase.

In the car, Jathrow let down the car windows and steam rolled out.

Minutes later, the car air conditioner strained, cranking out its usual workout.

A radio announcer spoke, "It is a hundred and ten degrees in the shade."

Jathrow sighed as he weaved through traffic. "It would be nice to be surfing right now." Jathrow parked outside a spacious Spanish-built house and checked the address. He quickened his steps and pushed the doorbell. The door opened where he was greeted by a beauty. She was someone he wouldn't mind being seen with in public. He tilted his head and with a smile, Jathrow offered his right hand. "Miss, I'm lost. I am looking for Hillary or an Irene Sill."

The woman opened the door wider, returning his smile. "You've found one of us. I'm Hillary, but I'm at a loss. And you are who?" She eyed him from head to toe.

"Sorry, Ms. Sill, I'm Jathrow Mowey, attorney for the client, Mr. Tom Glitching."

She raised her arms and said, "Oh, he's such a rat. That Mr. Tom Glitching is an overbearing, self-centered rich loser boy." She stomped her foot. "He thought money could buy him anything."

"May I be frank, Ms. Sills?"

Hillary motioned him to be seated. "Let me just tell you about our evening! Mr. Loser came in the hotel where my sisters and I were performing as show gals. And while doing our act, he sent us a note asking us to join him for a night in town. Here's the note." She sighed and handed him a piece of paper. "My sister, Blanch, was yet to perform a dance routine, and she agreed to catch up with us later. As for me, I had to come back for a scheduled dress rehearsal for the next day, a single act using my feathers."

Jathrow traced a finger inside the neck of his shirt and stood while glued watching her. Staying professional, he said, "Ms. Sill, I've come with information to share with you and your sisters. Are they here?"

Hillary stretched her long legs and walked down the hallway, stopping, and knocked lightly on two doors. Jathrow noticed only moment's later two carbon copies of Hillary walk into the room. Their one difference was their hair. Each was a shade lighter than the other.

"Well, Mr. Attorney," Hillary said with a drawl. "Pray tell us why you've come."

Jathrow squared his shoulders, airing with assertiveness and confidence. He opened the brown leather briefcase and handed each woman a copy outlining his client's wishes and the proposal. Jathrow flicked his blue-inked Rosewood pen and said, "Ladies, the amount of monies offered you for your night in town is very generous. One in which would be beneficial to each of you. My client, Mr. Tom Glitching, is not available and his father, Mr. John Glitching, has asked the firm to handle any unintentional upsets Mr. Tom Glitching may have caused." Jathrow raised a hand. "Furthermore, Mr. John Glitching demands your complete silence of your evening with his son. I'm offering in his stead the substantial amount of ten thousand dollars to each of you in the exchange for your honorable silence." He tapped his copy. "By signing these forms, you are not permitted to go public. Not on radio, TV, magazines, newspapers, or even in e-mails to friends. You are not to display any picture or pictures you may have acquired while with Mr. Tom Glitching. Ladies, do you understand? Don't fool yourself into trying for notoriety, for we wouldn't hesitate prosecuting any of you for breach of contract. Trust me when I say, we would win!"

Jathrow cupped his hands and rocked on his heels while waiting for the women's decision. His cell phone rang, and Jathrow walked into the foyer, breathing a frosty, "Hello?"

A sigh was uttered from Stan. He asked in his bass voice. "Did everything work out with the ladies?" Then he add, chuckling, "Or do I need to ask?"

"Let me get back with you on the matter." He closed the phone and rejoined the women. The corners of his mouth lifted.

Blanch handed him their signed forms.

Jathrow reached for the checkbook and handed them their check. "Thank you." He placed the signed forms in the brown leather briefcase, snapping it shut.

In the car, Jathrow used the on-voice command and called Stan. On the first ring, it was answered. "The forms are signed, and I'm on my way to deliver a copy to Mr. John Glitching." Jathrow crunched his brow when he heard Stan's laughter. Being irritated, Jathrow ended the call, but his phone rang again. The screen revealed Stan. "What!"

"Mr. John Glitching is in New York on another hunting investment, and he is expecting you there."

"I've just arrived from Virginia. I have plans for tonight."

"Your flight is arranged. You need to hurry. Your lift off is in two hours." There was a pause, and then Stan belted, "Remember your services are to be on twenty-four-hour call no matter what. That's why you get paid the big bucks!"

"So much for my life," Jathrow mumbled.

"Mr. John Glitching will have a date waiting for you. And the press with photographers will be swarming because of Mr. John Glitching's millions and your prestige being the best of the best. Man, will this generate publicity for us, so keep up the good work."

"But, Stan—"

"Jathrow, you're living every man's dream! You're powerful, single, and need I remind you—very wealthy. And in great demand. Now go go go!"

"I'm leaving! I'll call when I get back. Stan, we need to talk!"

Jathrow popped up the moonroof and breathed in the salty air. He sighed and placed a musical CD in the allotted slot. He willed himself to relax and continued to the airport, letting the music saturate his soul. He began humming.

There weren't any hitches with the flight from LA to New York. The plane ride went smooth and surprisingly on time. He rode in a cab and arrived at the hotel. Before joining Mr. John Glitching, Jathrow went into the men's shop and purchased a new shirt and silk tie. Then he checked into his suite and enjoyed a brief hot shower and shave. Jathrow enter the dining room where Mr. John Glitching was sitting. And sure enough, Mr. John Glitching had a date waiting for him.

The press and snappy photographers surrounded him. He was soon acknowledged by a bellowing voice, "Over here, Jathrow." Mr. John Glitching stood and stepped back from the table and waved.

Jathrow gave him a hearty slap on the back. And with outward arms, John chuckled and said, "Jathrow Mowey, this is my date, Ms. Julie Peep, and her friend, Ms. Donna Fair." Mr. John Glitching winked and added, "Mr. Jathrow Mowey has been my legal advisor for over twenty years, and he's the world's best attorney," he twitched his mustache, "in divorces. I should know, he has handled all seven of mine." Then he laughed.

The corners of Jathrow's mouth lifted, and the flash of bulbs began. After a few questions by the press, Jathrow reached for a chair and sat himself next to Ms. Donna Fair. He noticed pinkness appear on her face although the foursome conversations flowed throughout the meal. After an hour and fifty-five minutes, Jathrow placed his napkin on his plate and stood. He searched Mr. John Glitching's face and said, "It's been a long day, sir."

Mr. John Glitching scooted his chair back and held up four tickets. "Come on, old boy, the musical show is about to begin, and our evening is just beginning."

Jathrow glanced at the two ladies and then back at Mr. John Glitching. He let out a breath and walked with Mr. John Glitching while watching the ladies head toward the powder room.

The entertainment hostess came and showed Jathrow and Mr. John Glitching to their table.

The crowd cheered.

Jathrow stretched and was surprised to see Vivian. Her clingy agent, Mr. Samuel Gee, was escorting her. Vivian neared.

Jathrow saw her emerald eyes glitter and lock with his. He held his breath when she tiptoed and gave him a pecked on the cheek. She paused, allowing the flash of bulbs to continue. His hands were sweaty. He willed his legs to hold him up. Vivian had changed. She was the one in control. Placing a hand on his chest, she whispered, "It's good to see you." And leaned in for the camera.

Jathrow let out the held breath, watching Vivian walk away.

8

Mr. John Glitching nudged Jathrow and motioned to the waiting ladies to follow. After being seated, Donna Fair touched Jathrow's arm and said, "Time for the musical to begin." He nodded.

Jathrow looked in Vivian's direction, but the crowd surrounded her. However, Mr. Samuel Gee came in clear view. He slipped an arm around Vivian. The lights dimmed, and the curtain rose. Jathrow inhaled deeply, hunching his shoulders. *Another time, Vivian, another time.*

The audience began clapping; Jathrow adjusted his chair and watched the musical. Two hours later, the final curtain closed. Mr. John Glitching and Jathrow stood and talked with a few passersby; then they escorted the ladies into the hallway to retrieve their wraps. At the cloak counter, the men made small chitchat, and Jathrow handed over the signed documents resting in the manila envelope to Mr. John Glitching.

Mr. John Glitching patted his side jacket pocket and winked. Leaning in, he said, "Thanks, Jathrow. And now, my man, you are on your own. Ms. Donna Fair is an excellent companion, and she knows how to keep quiet." With a robust laugh, Mr. John Glitching clapped Jathrow on the shoulder and disappeared through the outside doors with his date dangling from his arm.

Jathrow caught Ms. Donna Fair's eye and held her wrap. They walked outside, where he hailed a cab. Jathrow yawned and shook his head. "I'm sorry, Ms. Fair." He hunched his shoulders and said, "Thanks for accompanying me tonight in the Big Apple, but the hour is late, and I still need to call in a report." He rubbed her arm and gave her a pleading look, then added, "I also have an early-morning flight back to LA. Thanks for understanding."

Ms. Donna Fair touched his cheek and only nodded. Jathrow stepped from the curb, opening the cab door, when another woman slid in front of Ms. Fair into the cab. His sky-blue eyes narrowed as he saw Vivian, alone.

She voiced, "Need a ride?"

"Thanks, Viv." He offered a helping hand to Ms. Fair and closed the cab door. He handed the driver some cash and waved bye to both women and watched the taillights fade into the night.

Back in the hotel room, Jathrow lifted the computer lid and powered up. He typed the information needed for Stan and an hour later hit the Send button. He stared at the computer then entered an inquiry: "Vivian Rose book tour."

A highlighted caption caught his eye: "Author Vivian Rose, Speaker / Book Signing—Australia. The famous actress Jacey Litten Rose is daughter to author Vivian Rose." He tapped the round table and checked the time. It was in the wee hours; he phoned Stan.

With a raspy voice, Stan asked, "Do you know what time it is?"

"Yes. I've called because I have a change of plans. Mark me absent from the office until further notice. I have some, um…personal business that needs my immediate attention."

"Why?" Stan asked. "You were just on a brief vacation in Virginia. And yes, you handled the fundraiser, but you also had several days off from work."

"Stan."

Stan cleared his throat and said, "I do appreciate your services at the fundraiser. However, Jathrow, when did anything in life mean more to you than work? Hello, Jathrow?"

Silence.

Jathrow called Jacey and left a voice message, asking her to call. Ten minutes later, his phone rang.

"This is Jacey."

Jathrow placed his hand in pocket and jingled his keys. "Hi, Jacey, thanks for calling so quickly." He cleared his throat. "I read online that your mother is scheduled to be in Australia for a book signing. Will she be staying with you?"

"Why, Uncle Jathrow," Jacey laughed, "it's good to hear from you too. And, yes, Mother will be here tomorrow."

Jathrow chuckled when Jacey referred to him as uncle. Jathrow said, "I'll 'uncle' you when I arrive."

Without changing clothes, Jathrow checked out from the New York hotel. Two hours later, in a cab, Jathrow sat glancing upward toward the stars, recalling the very first discussion he had with Jacey. She was only eighteen when they first talked. She had called his private cell number and introduced herself as Vivian Rose's daughter. She confessed to finding an old letter written to her mother, which included his cell number. Jacey wanted him to represent her in her business enterprises. He was amused at Jacey's spunk back then. She remained his Hollywood client until Jacey turned twenty-one. Jathrow shook his head. *I couldn't be more proud of Jacey than if she were my own daughter.* He eyes widened at the thought. *What? Now where did 'daughter' play into this?* He jerked open his cell phone and with voice command called the airport to change his flight arrangements.

"Hello, this is Jathrow Mowey. I need to cancel flight 425 to LA and book a flight to Australia. City? Sydney. Yes, round trip." He thought, *What am I doing?*

"Sir, I'm not able to find you a flight until Friday, and you will only be on standby. You know with the 2000 Olympics and all."

Jathrow's voice cracked, "I'll take it. Standby it is. Thanks." It was Tuesday at ten in the morning. He had the cab driver parked, and Jathrow darted into different New York men's stores, making purchases. Two and half hours later, his new luggage was packed with belts, socks, casual outerwear, personal items, and a Bible. He then added the two new suits—one blue and the other gray pinstripe. Jathrow placed the suitcases in the trunk of the cab. Two hours later, at the airport, Jathrow unloaded his luggage and proceeded inside. He stood in line another five hours, waiting for his standby Friday ticket. He hoped staying at the airport would get him an earlier flight. Jathrow found a bench and settled down. He removed his Italian-made jacket and loosened his silk tie. He adjusted and readjusted himself on the cement bench. He bunched his jacket under his head and finally slept with a hand glued to his luggage handles.

Jathrow opened an eye after feeling a sharp jab. He saw a man dressed in blue from the airline's security. It seemed only moments had passed since closing his eyes. It was 2:30 a.m. Wednesday morning. Jathrow bolted upright, causing a pain to shoot in his head. It throbbed. He asked security, "Can I help you?"

The security personal said, "See the woman at the counter? She has sent for you. There's been a cancellation for flight 243, and you're next in line."

Jathrow nodded and thanked the officer. He promptly toted his luggage to the counter. He straightened his tie and was amazed how his suit jacket showed very little wrinkles. Smiling, he handed over the flight ticket, and in return, she handed him his new agenda along with a note. He came aboard the flight and was pleasantly surprised to be seated in first class. He ordered coffee and a blueberry muffin. Then he gazed at the note: "I know who you are and it pleases me to help you. My name is Nan Tucket, and here's my cell number. If interested, call me anytime."

Jathrow crumpled the note and stuffed it into his jacket pocket. He took a sip of the treasured black coffee and smiled. *You've still got it, ole boy!*

The stewardess reached for his tray. "Would you like anything else?" She winked.

"I would. A pillow please." He was relieved when another male passenger called out for her help. Jathrow tilted his seat backward and closed his tired eyes. He settled in for the long trip of fifteen hours of flight ahead.

Jathrow blinked. The plane became jerky. He glanced out the side window as an announcement was made, "We've landed."

Jathrow stretched his legs, then shuffled from the plane. He walked to the luggage pickup area. While waiting, he checked his ticket package and noticed a reservation for a hotel suite had been overlooked. The luggage circled, and he grabbed both cases. He shrugged, then stepped inside the men's room. Jathrow unpacked several shaving articles and shaved his scruffy beard. Then he went to the airport's information counter.

"Hello, sir. May I help?"

Jathrow shifted and asked, "Are there any hotel rooms available on the island?"

She smiled. "You're in luck. I just received faxed information about an opening at the Crowne Plaza Hotel. Here's their phone number and location, Coogee Beach. But pardon me, sir," she whispered, "It's very expensive."

Jathrow winked and slid a few bills in her hand. "Thank you, miss." He reached inside his jacket pocket and retrieved his cell phone. "Hello, I would like to reserve a room." He could hardly hear the voice on the other end. The airport buzzed with excitement. He inhaled deep and breathed, "I know this is one of your busiest times, but I pay well." Jathrow transferred his things into his other hand and walked outside the airport building. He looked around before giving out his charge number. With a confirmation code, he rotated his shoulder and flagged a taxi. The cabbie opened his door and stored his luggage in the trunk.

"Where to, sir?"

"Crowne Plaza Hotel, please."

At the hotel, Jathrow was greeted with grandeur and was shown to his suite. He silently compared the suite to other places he had stayed and found it clean and spacious. The bellman unpacked Jathrow's luggage and waited. Jathrow signed and added a generous tip. He watched the gleam reach the bellman's face as he backed from the suite.

Jathrow walked into the luxurious bathroom, dropped his clothes, and reached for the shower knob. He stood enjoying the steamy water cascade over his head and run down his shoulders. Thirty minutes later, refreshed and dressed, Jathrow entered a restaurant. He ordered what usually took fifteen to twenty minutes to cook. A deep tiredness settled in his body. He thought, *Instead of feeling my active age of fifty-five, I feel like I'm 120 years old.*

Once in his deluxe suite, he stripped from his shirt and slacks and lay in bed. His eyes became heavy, and a deep, dreamless sleep took over.

Jathrow awaken to a loud rap on his door. He grabbed his slacks and swung open the door. Looking down, he saw a disturbed person standing there, shaking his hand. Jathrow hunched his shoulders and asked, "What?"

The short man identified himself as the hotel manager and shook an unpaid invoice in front of Jathrow's face. "Sir, yesterday's stay is not paid." And tapping the invoice, he added, "This is another day."

Jathrow rolled his eyes and pulled out his wallet. "Let me assure you, I made my payment for the suite over the phone. Here's the confirmation number."

Jathrow looked at the baffled manager and saw confusion in his dark brown eyes. Jathrow reached for his wallet and slid out his plastic, saying, "Here's for a week's stay."

The manager bowed and then spoke, "Mr. Mowey, I know who you are. We have many people coming and going from the hotel due to the Olympics, and I'm sorry. Enjoy your free breakfast."

Jathrow bit his bottom lip and stuffed a few bills in the manager's front shirt pocket. "Look, please don't announce my being here to anyone."

A photographer in the shadows of the hallway snapped pictures and ran. Jathrow followed, but the man disappeared.

Once inside the suite, Jathrow decided to go surfing. The sea was the one place where he could think. And this he needed before a visit with Jacey and, hopefully, Vivian. He had lost two days in traveling, so what was one more day. The warm water was crystal blue and clear. The waves seemed promising. The day for the board was good as he rode the waves. The waters beckoned him time and again.

The evening sun disappeared over the painted horizon, and the breeze stirred the air. Jathrow returned the rented board and chuckled when people offered bids for it. In front of the hotel, Jacey's manager met him. "Mr. Jathrow Mowery, Jacey asked me to hand-deliver this. I'm not used to waiting." She turned and left.

In the suite, Jathrow tossed his key and wallet on the nightstand. He took a quick shower. Then he reached for the sealed note from Jacey and changed his mind about dining out. He removed his tie and jacket and sat down. At the table he read,

> Hello, my uncle. In regards to your question, yes, my mother will be staying with me. I'm on holiday for the week. If you swing by the public library Wednesday, Mom's agent, Mr. Samuel Gee, will announce where and when mother's next book signing will take place. Mother is also scheduled for a two-hour reading and book signing there. Perhaps she will listen and hear you out. However, I'm not permitted to mention your name. What did you do, Jathrow?

As he stood, he heard a light tap at the door. His evening meal had arrived. Jathrow signed the bill, adding a hefty tip. The bellman's eyes bulged. He said, "Sir, if there is anything you need during your stay, my name is Bill Owens." He bowed and added, "Thank you." He closed the door.

Jathrow anticipated a great seafood meal, but it might as well been rubber. Thoughts on what was left unspoken between Vivian and him rushed in. Jathrow reached for his trusty Bible and read in Psalms 27. "The Lord is my strength." Receiving comfort, he prayed. Jathrow became a great believer in the Word, but his life hadn't always demonstrated it. He sense another prayer might help. He ventured to the balcony and bowed his head, "Creator, grant me wisdom, especially where Vivian is concerned. My confidence is shattered, and our friendship is in jeopardy. Lord, I really don't know why. Help me out here."

The phone rang, which made Jathrow jump. Hurriedly, he said, "Hello?"

"Jathrow Mowey, what are you doing in Australia?"

"David, David Fleck, is that you, friend?"

"Yes, it is. I saw your picture on the news this morning. You were at the airport. I also read where people were bidding on a surf board you rented." He cleared his throat. "However, our friend Vivian called me two days ago. She is upset at how you left her at the fund raiser for another woman."

"What? I left? I don't think so." Jathrow blew air through his lips. "David, remember? I told you before I left Virginia while we were on the beach how Vivian waltzed from the fundraiser with Walter, her decease husband's friend. Need I say again, I was stranded with Nurse Betty."

David snorted. "Jathrow, Vivian doesn't see it your way. Your friendship, my friend, is in the toilet."

Jathrow willed his fisted hands to his sides. "This is not funny, but thanks for the heads-up."

David said, "Us men must stick together. Good luck, friend. I'm rooting for you." Then the phone lines went silent.

Jathrow sat down and placed his head in his hands. How was he ever going to straighten things out between him and Vivian? And her low opinion of him. *How could she possible think I would ever ditch her for Nurse Betty?* He paced the floor. "What a mess! What must I say or do?" He looked upward. *Lord, help me!*

His cell phone rang.

"Have you worked things out with Vivian?" It was Richard Sr.

He grunted, "No. How am I ever going to mend our broken fences?"

There was a long pause. "Jathrow, you wine and dine the finest women all over the world. What's wrong with you? This is our friend Vivian. Just ask her to listen. Then tell her the truth about that evening with Nurse Betty at the fundraiser. Send her candy, flowers, or invite her out to an opera or a play. Use your charm. But most of all, be honest."

"I don't understand why Vivian took my attention with Nurse Betty so personal. Richard Sr., I had to protect Nurse Betty from being the latest news gossip victim. I didn't want her to be a spectacle because of her misguided actions." He sighed. "Richard Sr., how could Vivian even think I was womanizing that night?"

"Well, Jathrow, you always had the model-looking women dangling from your arm. So what do you expect?"

Jathrow inhaled deep. "I've always enjoyed women, but never at Vivian's expense. I care for her, and I value our friendship."

Richard Sr. said, "Jathrow, what's wrong with you? It seems you have a narrow sight issue. Look within yourself. I do believe you really want a different kind of relationship to happen between you and Vivian. Your feelings run deeper than even you realize. I've got to go. Chloe is calling."

Jathrow called the lobby and inquired for Bill Owen. He ordered green tea and toast with grape jelly on the side. Within moments, a rap came on the door. Jathrow handed the bellhop a sum of money. Bill said, "Thanks, sir! Call me anytime."

Jathrow powered up the computer and verified he was the hometown news. He found the picture and information David and Richard Sr. had indicated about his presence in Australia. He pushed from the chair and ran his hands through his long hair. "You've done it again, Jathrow."

9

Jathrow paced the sidewalk. He couldn't bring himself to face Vivian at the library. His stomach flip-flopped at just the thought. Earlier, he had seen Vivian's flyers posted in storefront windows announcing where her book signing was to be held. Jathrow had bought a double arrangement of pink roses and had purchased a box of caramel chocolates. *She'll see me now.* His heart fluttered.

The street crowd was impossible. He dodged bobbing people coming in and out of street-lined shops, apparently looking for tokens with the Olympic Ring symbol. But he whistled, happiness emerging within step by step. He would see Vivian. However, she believed he shunned her for another woman. His stomach again twisted in those familiar knots. Now each step closer to Stadium, where Vivian was to do a reading, became heavier, and Jathrow felt ill. He glanced at the flowers and candy he was carrying. Vivian wasn't the regular run-of-the-mill woman. He dumped the chocolates and trashed all but five roses in the street's trash container.

He had reached the Stadium Australia, and the crowds were on their feet cheering and clapping, awaiting Vivian Rose's appearance. Jathrow smiled at the pleasure she must feel with the worldwide success of another novel. He knew Vivian was passionate about her writing even when they were in high school. New heights of roar lifted from the crowd. Jathrow was proud of his lifelong friend. Everyone loved her.

A soft hand rested on Jathrow's shoulder.

He turned, and shock registered on his face. The all-too-familiar perfume wafted through the air.

"Jathrow what are you doing lollygagging in the gateway?" Jacey hooked her arm with his, and they bobbed through the crowd.

Jathrow waited until they were somewhat alone. "Thanks for rescuing me at the gateway, Jacey. I was deep in thought." He squared shoulders and asked, "Will you hand-deliver these five roses and note to your mother?"

The crowd sounded louder. He glanced over the stadium. It was packed. The overhead sign featured, "American Author, Vivian Rose." He slipped into the side wing and watched Vivian and her response when her name was announced.

She licked her lips and shivered. Mr. Gee patted her arm, giving his crooked smile. Then he asked, "Ready to meet your fans?"

Jathrow held his breath.

Vivian watched Jacey step from behind the curtain. She handed her pink roses with a note. Then she whispered into her mother's ear. Vivian glanced around and spotted Jathrow.

He waved and silently hoped his Italian-made suit and long blond hair would still appeal to her. They locked eyes, and he noticed Vivian's green eyes were cold, and he didn't know what to make of it. His stomach twisted in knots.

Her agent nudged Vivian's arm. She straightened and stepped forward.

The audience whistled and cheered even more. Vivian folded into a chair, adjusted the microphone, and cleared her throat. "Hello, everyone." She motioned the people to sit down. She began reading.

The advocate readers were on edge. After thirty minutes, she closed the book. The people clapped and yelled, "Read on!"

Vivian stood, bowed, then said, "Ladies and gentlemen, thank you." She motioned for her agent.

A display table was ushered in with stacks of her newly released novel. Vivian sat with pen in hand. Her daughter came alongside her. The crowd cheered. Cameras flashed. Jacey bent and kissed her mother. Holding out a copy of her mother's book, she said, "Sign my copy, Mother."

The ushers contained the crowd. Mr. Samuel Gee stepped in and announced, "Men and women, please form two lines. Our author will be happy to sign your book ."

Over three thousand fans received novels. Some copies were personally signed while other copies purchased were prestamped by Vivian Rose. Hours passed. Finally, alone with her agent and Jacey, the curtains dropped. Only Jathrow was still standing in the wings. He was thumbing his lapel, waiting. Vivian smelled the roses and with quick steps moved to his side. His breath caressed her face. She stepped back. Now in tears, she said, "Thank you for the five roses."

He whispered, "You remembered."

She nodded. Cleared her throat, "Of course, Jathrow, I remember. Each rose stands for a single friend, which makes us five souls joined together always forever."

Jathrow held his breath, waiting for her to say more, but she turned. He reached for Vivian's hand; things were left unsettled between them, but her reliable agent intervened. From the corner of his misty eye, Jathrow saw Jacey biting her lip.

Jathrow whispered, "Please, Vivian, have dinner with me. We can go somewhere casual where you want."

She paused.

"Sydney Tower Restaurant? I hear their buffet is awesome. We could enjoy the bird's eyeview." Jathrow lifted his head and arched his brows as he waited for her answer.

Vivian moved around Mr. Gee and reached and squeezed Jathrow's hand. Her bottom lip quivered a little. "All right. Stop by Jacey's trailer at nine o'clock tonight. I'll be ready." She held the roses under her nose.

Jathrow threw a look over to Jacey and mouthed, "Thank you."

Vivian was pacing when the cab pulled up.

They rode in silence to the restaurant, and between them, chilliness set in. The restaurant was busy but not crowded. They sat at a table with a panoramic view of the city. They sipped on their iced tea while waiting for the buffet bar to get restocked. Jathrow made an effort to talk, but Vivian stared out the window. When they went to the buffet bar, they selected a huge amount of seafood. However, he noticed Vivian pushed her food from side to side, not really taking a bite. And his food tasted like cotton. Jathrow was glad for the iced tea.

Vivian spoke, "The flowers given were a lovely and thoughtful gesture." She snapped and adjusted her napkin on her lap. "Shame on you if you thought you needed to come to Australia and explain your behavior in Virginia." She plunked down her fork and pointed a shaking index finger.

"Jathrow, I understand. You are a carefree man and are very magnetic to women. What we share between us is strictly friendship." Vivian blotted her mouth. "I left with Walter, a friend of my late husband, when his date, at your greeting, ended up in your arms on the dance floor."

A cameraman squatted in front of their table and snapped a picture. Vivian smiled, then excused herself from the table. Jathrow nodded and stood. She departed toward the powder room. Jathrow placed his hands on his narrow hips, watching. As he was pulling out his seat to sit down, Jacey rushed to the table with two tall thin model-looking blondes. Jathrow held their chairs and then took a seat. Vivian came back and sat down.

"Hello, Mother." Jacey stretched out her hand and said, "Tammy, Sheryl, meet, Vivian Rose." Turning her head, she added, "And this is the world-renowned attorney, Jathrow Mowery."

He nodded.

"My friends are only in town for a few hours."

Vivian stood and greeted each model. Jathrow followed suit with his eyebrows arched.

The ladies shook Vivian's hand and then turned their eyes toward Jathrow.

They giggled. Vivian gave a nod to her daughter. Jacey lifted from her chair and gave Jathrow a big hug and kiss, causing a distraction.

Unknown to Jathrow, Vivian had texted her daughter for intervention. *There's something different about my feelings that are surfacing for Jathrow. And it's confusing me. I needed to escape. I feel it may be more than a friendship, and I will not make a fool of myself again.* Without another word, Vivian edged her way through the restaurant's door and found Jacey's green convertible coop car. She saw her suitcases were in the backseat. Bittersweet tears streamed down Vivian's cheeks. She drove blindly down the highway, replaying the forgiveness speech she offered Jathrow and felt pleased she hadn't given into her true desire for him. She would thank Jacey later for her help .

Vivian glanced at the car dash and saw the hour. She had driven over a hundred miles; her eyes were heavy and felt strained. She pulled into a roadside rest and glanced over the surroundings. Vivian hurried and removed a blanket from the trunk and slid back into the car. A truck driver gave her a nod. She locked both doors, then pulled forward under a security light and rested her eyes, and sleep invaded.

A horn sounded nearby, and her eyes fluttered open. The truck driver peered out his driver's window and yelled, "Good morning, miss. I'm heading out. Sorry, it's so early, but I must make my way before the roads become busy. Where you headed?"

"I'm going home—America."

The truck driver rustled around the back of his seat and waved a map. He swung with ease to the ground and walked over to her. "If you follow this route, gas, food, and roadside rests are along the way. He winked and tipped his cap. "Ma'am, traveling the back roads is safe, but be careful, and good luck. I recognized you, Ms. Rose, for my wife collects your books." Tipping his cap, he smiled and once again seated himself behind the big eighteen-wheeler.

"Wasn't that man kind. I'm glad he didn't pry." She tended to morning necessities and followed the map. Well into the afternoon, the sun scorched down, causing the air conditioner to run hot. Vivian's eye flitted, her stomach growled, and she needed to use the ladies' facility. "Wow. Finally there's a truck stop ahead."

Vivian took her time and ordered the breakfast special, two eggs, hash browns, toast, and black coffee. She ordered a large coffee to go, paid her bill, then pushed from the table. She patted her stomach and in the car, said, "They sure served a trucker's meal."

A parcel hotel sign on her left appeared. She parked and watched people come and go. Vivian grabbed her pink floppy hat and pushed her red hair underneath. She checked in and signed in under a phony name and paid in cash.

The vacant room set way in the back. It was small and appeared clean. Vivian called, requesting a wakeup call at 6:00 a.m. She tossed her hat on a rack and reached in her bag, and out came her nightclothes. After showering, Vivian pulled out her cell phone and called, "Mr. Samuel Gee, you need to know I left for the USA!" She hung up.

Vivian recalled that Mr. Samuel Gee had surprised her right before Jathrow showed up for their dinner date. He had said, "Vivian, I've stopped by because I would like us to take our relationship to the next level. From professional to an intimate one."

Vivian mouth had dropped open. He had wanted to be more than her agent. At that moment she did think of his attributes. Mr. Samuel Gee was honest and trustworthy; however, his thin lips reminded her too much of her late husband. She just couldn't commit to him on a personal level! Although as a man, Samuel was undeniable desirable. He was a savvy dressed and had a toned body for a man of sixty-seven years and was very tall. It grieved her to see Samuel's disappointment when she said no. No to a marriage proposal.

Her cell phone rang, making her jumped. She saw Jacey's name. "Hello, baby girl. Did you get in much of a pickle helping me escape from Jathrow?"

"What happened to you Vivian?" Vivian gasped. It was Jathrow. His voice broke and became raspy, "I thought we were at an understanding and were headed in a returned friendship. I didn't expect a runaway tactic from you. Vivian, dear, where are you? Let me come to you." Jathrow paused and added in a whisper, "Viv, I need to tell you how I feel—Vivian? Vivian?" The lines were silent.

She became startled when her cell phone rang again. Vivian did not answer and let it roll into voicemail. She viewed the cell screen moments later as it rang and saw the caller was Samuel Gee. She dabbed her eyes and answered the phone guiltily, "Yes, Samuel."

"You left because I asked you to marry me?"

"Samuel! Please, I had other reasons." She tapped the cell phone. "I'll see you in the states. I need space. I will call you when I am ready to talk."

"Vivian."

"I'm hot on the writings of a new manuscript. I don't want to be disturbed." Drawing a quick breath, she said, "Thanks for juggling my schedule. Have a safe flight I'll be in touch soon. Bye."

"All right, Vivian. I'll wait for your call. Bye."

Vivian's cell phone buzzed several times, but she didn't dare answer. She clicked off her cell phone and placed it on its charger.

A knock came at the door. Vivian jerk. Giving herself a stern lecture, she asked, "Who's there?"

"Doorman. Here with your complementary evening tray."

She opened the door an inch, then motioned for him to enter.

He set the dinner tray down, and she walked with him to the door and handed him a big tip. Then she bolted the lock. While nibbling, she flipped through the TV channels and found an old favorite movie, *You've Got Mail.* The TV flickered, and her eyelids drooped. She moved the snack tray aside and slipped into bed, covering with a sheet. She tossed and turned and thoughts of Jathrow's sexy voice threatened her. She sat up, hit her pillow, and willed herself to lie back down. Once again a restless sleep invaded.

There was a peculiar ringing sounded. Vivian hesitated but forced herself to pick up the receiver. She laughed when the automated voice screeched, "Wake up. This is your morning service call." She reached for her robe as someone rapped on the door. A man's voice said, "Doorman. Breakfast is served complements of the house."

"Thank you. Please leave the tray outside my door." She listened as the footsteps tapered away. Vivian retrieved the tray, ate, and got ready to leave. She viewed the trucker's map and realized a speedy drive was needed if she was to purchase a ticket and board the ferry by 10:30 a.m. Vivian slung her things in the huge bag and poured black coffee into the foam cup she retrieved from the car. She flipped the cell phone on, and it rang in an instant. "Hello!"

"It's Jacey. Sorry about Jathrow. He used my cell phone. He had hoped you would call me. He's troubled over your leaving. And admitted to me he cares about you."

Vivian sighed. "Jacey, I'm boarding my passage home. Glad you called. I've made arrangements in getting your vehicle back to you. Thanks for the loaner."

"Mother, I hope you know what you're doing. Jathrow left right after you did for his home in California. He's really sad. Mom, sometimes feelings aren't only a one-way street. Why don't you make the first move? Let him know how you really feel!"

"Jacey, let it go. He wants us to only have a friendship, and well, I'm not sure that's enough anymore."

"Mom, he's successful, handsome, and so free."

Vivian cleared her throat, "Jacey great reviews on your movie. You're remarkable. I'll call you after I'm home. Bye, sweetheart. I love you."

Being the flights were all booked, she decided to just leave by any means. After eleven days aboard the floating craft, Vivian finally stepped foot on USA soil in Florida. She cried, thinking of her loss of what she and Jathrow could have shared. She willed her emotions down.

At the cottage a few days later, she carried through with her writing on a new adventure. And two weeks later, Vivian woke to a bright sunny morning, and the breeze felt warm. She needed to prune the roses and plant more flower bulbs. Vivian headed to the shed and slipped on her gardening gloves and flopped on her pink oversized hat. She rolled her tool cart over to the flowerbeds. Several hours later, sweat trickled down her face. She fanned with her hat, then returned to the outer beds, raked, and trimmed the shrubs. Vivian paused and cupped her hands around her eyes, for the sun's rays were blinding. There were her friends, Ty and David, in the parked truck.

"Vivian," David called. He flung the truck door open and jumped down. Upon approaching, he grabbed Vivian into a bear hug. Ty joined them.

David said, "Richard Sr. asked me to stop by and see if you were home from being abroad. He's needing a garden party setting for Jacey and Richard Jr., and he wants to hold the party here at the cottage."

Vivian motioned for them to sit.

"Richard Sr. has been calling you, and when there wasn't any answer, he called us. Ty and I volunteered to come right over. "How was your book tour?"

Vivian removed her hat and wiped her brow. "It's good to see you both. The tour was cut short, and that's all I intend to say. Now why and when did Richard Sr. want a party? And does Jacey know about this?"

"Of course, Jacey knows. Richard Sr. also mentioned Jacey had texted and e-mailed you when she couldn't reach you by house phone. Have you, er, checked your e-mail?"

10

Vivian looped her arm with each of her friends, "Well, men," she said, "let's move from the sun and go sit in the shade."

David nodded and excused himself. He came carrying a snack and beverage from the truck. "Leftovers from another party."

"Who would have thought Richard Jr. would fly halfway around the world and then pursued a relationship with Jacey." Ty's eyebrows arched. "Not that Jacey isn't worthy. She is." His face went red.

Vivian folded her hands, snickering. "While I was in Australia, Jacey mentioned that Richard Jr. had bumped into her at the art museum. With both their interest in art, they decided to attend an art class together." Vivian fanned herself. "When Jacey spoke of Richard Jr., her blue eyes brightened. They held that special sparkle."

David refilled their glasses with his special orange juice and said, "It will be nice having Jacey back home with us again."

"I hear RCA Movie Production is pursuing her in making films here." Ty said.

Vivian set her glass on the cement table. "I'm glad she's returning home." And ignored any mention of filmmaking. "Richard Jr. is a good guy. He's steady and reliable." Vivian reached for Ty and David's arm, then they resumed walking. After entering the cottage, she broke arms with the men and walked to her desk, picking up a writing pad. She said, "David, make a list. What about board games, yard games, and think about including some young entertainment. Maybe Latin flavor music and of course your great food selection."

David nodded. "I'm on it. Oh, Richard Sr. is on his way. I called him and let him know you're back from being abroad. He wants in on the plan."

Richard Jr. entered into the cottage front door along with his father. In a rumbling voice, he said, "Vivian." Richard Sr. bent down and gave her a hug. "When is Jacey arriving? I haven't read my e-mails." Vivian said.

Wide crinkles formed at Richard Sr.'s mouth, which broadened his round face. He said, "Jacey's e-mail indicated her arrival is set for next month on the seventh. So do we want the engagement party the weekend of her arrival?"

David thumbed his calendar and said, "September 10, which is a Friday, works for me. Let's say 6:00 p.m." He reached for the pencil behind his ear.

Vivian nodded. "Sure, why not."

She turned toward Ty. "I need your cleaning services again, before and after the party. I want the complete cleaning package, with wall washing, paint touch-ups, floors polish, and carpet scrub."

Ty said, "You can count on me."

Vivian tapped the seat for Richard Sr. and his son to sit. "Will you help in addressing the invitations?" Then she stared at Richard Jr. "Are you sure about my daughter? You know with the forever-after stuff?" She fluffed her handkerchief. "I don't want either of you to be hurt."

Richard Jr. said, "Vivian, I'm sure. I've prayed about my decision and am at peace."

She touched his cheek and nodded.

"I spoke with Mother and Father before contacting the minister." He cleared his throat. "You know I've always loved Jacey even when she was a mud-pie-making kid. I'm twelve years older than she is, and I had to wait until she grew up to pursue her dreams. My life's work is much like Dad's, dealing with figures. I know it's not the most exciting field, however, I've invested in the market and have saved ample money. Matter of fact, Jacey can have me sign a prenuptial agreement and keep all her assets from her movies." Not batting an eye, he stated, "Mrs. Rose, I'm an honorable man, and I truly love Jacey!"

His dad clapped him on the back. "I'll bring my wife over tomorrow if that's all right. She can help with the engagement invitations and the addressing of envelopes."

"Friends, enough talk about the party. Since we are together, let's play a friendly game of dominos. Like old times." David looked around the room.

They set the card table in the living room, and the game was on. Several hours passed. Vivian chuckled as she watched Ty for the third time win the game.

He shook his head and said, "Can you believe this? I don't usually win at anything."

Vivian patted his arm. "Ty, I'm speaking for all of us. You're a great family man. A real winner in our book." She kissed his cheek.

❧

The days and weeks passed. And on the day of the party, Vivian examined each orchid arrangement and saw they were healthy, in full bloom, in rainbow colors. She smiled how Ty had moved the cottage furniture to make allowance for dancing.

Jacey's smile showed in her eyes while holding hands with Richard Jr. Both appeared so happy. Richard Jr. just rocked back and forth on his heels waiting for their wonderful announcement.

David watched as servers carry the selected trays of pigs in a blanket, small circular sausages, and variable cheese appetizers throughout the rooms.

David approached Vivian, "Vivian does everything meet with your approval?"

Vivian batted at his hand, "You've really out done yourself this time." Vivian pointed over the heads of the people as they arrived and asked, "Where did you find this lively band? You know, people will ask."

David whispered, "From the Internet." He rocked back and forth on his shoes, nodding his head. David extended an arm for Vivian, and they took a moment and walked outside. She gasped at the sight. "David, it's so magical. However did you wrap the flowers around the columns?"

"You and the guests will be able to watch the setting of monarch butterflies free. They'll flutter all around the patio."

"Ah, David, perfect!"

The dance area began filling with people. Before David excused himself to oversee the evening's work, he lean in, "My friend, may I have this dance?"

Vivian glanced at his wife, Doreen, who nodded her approval. David removed his serving jacket and handed it to his wife. After all, they were childhood friends, and they could step aside from traditional protocol. Vivian gazed into his beaming face and replied, "On one condition. You use both feet on the dance floor and stay off mine."

David grabbed her hand and twirled her around the floor. On the next song, Vivian danced with her late husband's friend and was relieved when Ty cut in. "May I have this dance?" As the two whirled the room, Ty said, "Jacey looks like she is floating on air. She is so beautiful, just like you, inside and out."

Vivian elbowed Ty. "You old flatterer. No wonder your wife and girls enjoy being with you. You're kind and thoughtful."

The bandleader clapped his hands to quiet the crowd. He motioned for Richard Sr. and Chloe to come on stage. Then he motioned to Vivian.

She only hesitated for a minute before heading toward the stage.

Vivian searched the crowd for the one person she had secretly hoped would be in attendance. To her disappointment, the long blond hair, electric blue-eyed Jathrow was a no-show. She shouldn't been surprised, for he hadn't answered the invitation. She glanced at the wooden floor. *I was wrong again in thinking something could actually happen between the two of us. Jathrow is just a tease like he was all those years ago.*

Ty nudged Vivian's shoulder. "Come back to the party, friend." He arched a brow. "It appears Jathrow couldn't make it tonight."

Vivian gave Ty a fisted punch and said, "Jathrow could have been here. I had hope for Jacey's sake he would come." She bit her lower lip.

Ty said, "Don't look now, but—"

Someone blew on Vivian's neck and whisked her away. She heard the wonderful crooning voice say, "You don't have to wish any longer, friend, I'm here. Let the party begin!"

Vivian swayed. He looked so debonair in his black tux . She tripped and fell into his strong arms. Jathrow's breath tickled her ear as he whispered, "Do I need to do resuscitation to you again like when we went for a swim?" His eyebrows slanted, and a slight curve slid to his mouth.

"Jathrow, how, when, where did you come from?"

His arm cupped her closer, and a chuckle escaped him. He said, "Look." And nodded for her to see Richard Sr. and Chloe were waiting and motioning for her on stage. In the excitement, Richard Sr. announced the engagement of his son to Jacey. Jathrow whispered, "They're calling for you." He wiggled through the crowd, excusing them. He helped Vivian on stage, and he handed her the flowers to present to her daughter. Vivian bit her bottom lip as she glanced over the crowd and locked eyes with Jathrow. A second or two passed before she caught him winking at her. Vivian made a short speech, adding her blessings for Jacey and husband-to-be, Richard Jr. Then Vivian stepped aside .

Jacey, in her slender stature, stood with her intended, admiring her perfect ten-pointed Topaz engagement ring. He placed a hand out and led Jacey onto the dance floor where the officially engaged couple's first dance began. And the crowd roared.

Vivian heard Jathrow whistling over everyone. The onlookers cheered congratulations and some yelled, "Way to go, Jacey!"

Richard Sr. with Chloe joined their son on the dance floor and exchanged dance partners. After the song ended, Richard Jr. bowed and danced with Vivian. Stepping in for Jacey's deceased father, Jathrow stepped forward, bowed, and whirled Jacey on the dance floor.

The dance ended, and Vivian was face-to-face with Jathrow. Her green eyes widened, and she licked her lips. It was the next dance—hers and Jathrow's. The music slowed, and only the people's feet were shuffling back and forth. Vivian slipped off her fringed wrap and curtsied, and Jathrow bowed. Vivian placed her hand in his. He placed a hand on her back and edged his fingers downward where the V-shape on the dress had dropped just above her bottom. Vivian removed her hand from his and placed it on his chest. She felt heat. She struggled with her strained emotions. Jathrow leaned in and whispered, "You're breathtaking." He pulled Vivian closer. His breath was warm. She could do nothing but lay her head on his shoulder. The photographer snapped pictures. Vivian's head arose, but Jathrow nuzzled and twirled with the music. Jathrow said, "Don't run from me again, Viv. We need to talk." Jathrow then dipped Vivian backward.

Jathrow bent and brushed her lips lightly. He was interrupted and whisked away to dance with other women, but his narrow blue eyes searched until he found Vivian. Her look lingered, and he winked. Jathrow charmed others, but after the sixth dance, he waved off the women holding their dance cards and said, "Sorry, ladies, I'm no longer available." Nodding, he walked to Vivian. His blue eyes gleamed. He spoke, "I'm one lucky man to be added to your dance card." He bowed and reached for her hand once again.

Vivian shivered and waltzed along with the music. Jathrow only left her side once to retrieve punch for them. And she watched him make his way through the crowd. He squared his broad shoulders and swaggered. Jathrow appeared so assured of himself. Vivian slid a hand through her hair and muttered, *What's wrong with me? Remember, he isn't safe.* She breathed a rushed prayer, *Dear Lord, You know I've always loved Jathrow.* Then she bit her bottom lip. *Shall I take a chance?*

Jathrow came near and warmed her skin as their shoulders grazed each other's.

Ty and David both approached Vivian. "Vivian, will you escort us into the kitchen." David took Vivian's arm, leaving Ty standing alone with Jathrow. David cornered Vivian. "Are you all right? You're acting weird. It's like you don't know who Jathrow really is." He touched her quivering chin. "You know Jathrow has never been a one-woman kind of man and certainly not a staying kind either! Oh, Vivian, you know we love him and we enjoy his company, but he is what he is. When it comes to his reputation, it precedes him about women. He loves them and leaves them." David shielded Vivian for a moment longer from Jathrow's view and placed a hand on her shoulder, "I don't want to see you hurt all over again."

Vivian squirmed, "David, stay out of this. I'm a grown woman, and it's between Jathrow and me."

David didn't budge, and he held Vivian with both hands while he spoke, "Listen to me, Vivian. We've been friends since grade school. I declare if you obviously think Jathrow has changed, let him prove it to all of us. We'll stand by you as we always have, and we'll be here to pick up the pieces should he leave you. In case you have forgotten, that's what real friends do. We love and protect one another unconditionally."

Vivian's mouth opened then closed as Jacey walked in to the kitchen and said, "Mother, let's take a walk in the garden."

Vivian accepted her daughter's invitation, and both nodded to the people as they spoke their thank-you for coming to the engagement party and their good-byes for some were leaving. Arm in arm, daughter and mother strolled. They came where the cement table and bench were webbed among the different colored pineapple grass. As they sat, winter daisies and Russian sage also surrounded them. The moment was wonderful. Vivian patted her daughter's hand. "Dear, I'm glad you're home, and I couldn't be happier with your decision about your future husband."

Jacey giggled and blushed. "Mother, first I want to thank you for the splendid party you've given my Richard and me." She held up a hand to stop her mother from speaking. "My Richard and I remind me of you and Jathrow. I know you have questions about him, but why not take a leap of faith and explore your feelings. He could maybe be more than a friend." Jacey stood. "Jathrow called me and admitted he's confused about his feelings on the two of you. He said no other woman has ever had affected him as you do." She kissed her mother's cheek, "Ah, Mom, go for it. Throw caution and care to the wind. I believe he is worth it. Secretly, I've also been praying for the two of you."

Vivian hugged her daughter. Jacey requested to return to the party. But Vivian stayed behind. Should she give Jathrow a chance? Would she be the one hurt and be the laughingstock like David indicated. Vivian glanced toward the incoming footsteps. It was Jathrow. She weakened as he came near. She loved his long blond hair. She stood and inhaled the night's freshness and hesitated before taking a step. Jathrow's smile engulfed her as he came near. He nudged her a little closer, and his hands were warm. She felt his breath and gazed up and saw his full lips were close enough to touch, and she went dizzy.

Vivian heard voices as if they were floating around her. As she opened her eyes, she realized she was lying in her bed. David, Ty, Richard Sr., and Jathrow were staring down at her. Jacey placed a cold towel on Vivian's forehead and was patting her hand. "Oh, Mother, you're back."

11

Vivian blinked and shakily asked, "What happened?"David knelt with a bowl of chicken broth. Jacey helped with propping her mother up. David asked, "Have you eaten anything at all today?"

Vivian shook her head and said, embarrassed, "No."

David let out a muffled oath, then said, "Now sip this."

Vivian obeyed. She hiccupped and motioned Jacey close. She whispered, "I'm all right now, and I want to be left alone. Will you show all my friends out? You need to join Richard Jr. But let Jathrow know he may call me later. Only not where a soul can hear. Promise?"

Jacey nodded while smiling. "All right." She turned and motioned the men to follow her into the next room. "Let Mother rest for now."

Vivian watched as Jacey looped arms with Jathrow. He nodded, and a boyish smile appeared on his face. She knew he would call soon. Vivian heard Jacey thank the men for making this day so special. She offered to help clean up from the party as Richard Jr. stood near, but the men cheerfully waved them on.

An hour or so later, Vivian came to the kitchen. The engaged couple and guests had left, including Jathrow. She felt stronger. Only David and Ty were bustling around picking up this and carrying that to the truck.

A few minutes later, Vivian spoke with them, paid them, and then they left. She took advantage of the peace and quiet and rested for the next few days but wondering why no word came from Jathrow.

Exactly three weeks later, and after breakfast, Vivian walked in the flower garden with pad and pen in hand where she plotted a new romance story. By midday, the characters penned came alive. Vivian laid the pad and pen down clapping her hands. Pride burst forth as she felt moved deep within her soul, for this writing was not like any other of her novels.

A familiar voice caught her attention. "Can anyone join this private party of delighted happiness?"

Vivian in awe opened her arms, allowing Jathrow to step in and embrace her. She experienced his delightful manly scent. She stood and looked intently into his dark blue eyes. They seemed to reflect an unusual vulnerability, and then Jathrow took a step backward. She shivered and blinked while asking herself inwardly, *Had his eyes really changed?* She shivered again for the questionable smoky hue had vanished and only a cold icy blue was staring back. Jathrow slipped a hand in his trouser pocket and once again appeared self-assured and relaxed as the old friend she knew long ago. He asked, "Do you have any coffee made?"

She smiled and nodded. "Come, follow me."

In the living room, Jathrow was seated with her photo album.

He thumbed through the pages and paused when seeing an old picture of Vivian in her teens. He smiled. Entering the room, Vivian handed him a steaming mug and noticed him looking at the photo. "Jathrow, it was a long time ago."

He set the cup on the coffee table and fingered the photo. Not looking up, he said softly, "You haven't changed. You're still beautiful and the most kind, honest person I've ever known."

Vivian felt herself blush. "You've always had a way with words even when you were in high school as a beanpole boy."

He threw his head back and heartily laughed.

Vivian continued, "I do think having the long blond locks and your blue eyes didn't hurt you."

He closed the photo album and searched her face. "Viv, I need to tell you something. I'm bringing my law practice here to Richmond. I've spoken and met with Richard Sr. and the realtor. You remember Old Man Pretcher?"

Vivian's smile faded. She dropped her hands into her lap. "Why move here now?"

He rolled his eyes. "There's more I need to say, but first, will you have dinner with me tonight so we can talk or you just listen?" He stood and paced the floor. "It isn't that I can't talk now, but over dinner would be nicer. Well?"

After releasing a long breath, Vivian said, "Take me in to town. We can shop at the Piggly Wiggly. I'll fix the dinner for the both of us. It will be more private."

The corner of his lips lifted. "Want to go now? I'll fix a salad."

On the ride into town, they joked and joshed with one another like time had stood still. At the store, Jathrow handed the cart over to Vivian. She had always barked out orders to what he could and couldn't put in the cart.

When they reached home, he carried in the groceries and set them on the kitchen counter. Vivian reached for two aprons and handed him one. She laughed at his easiness in the kitchen. Little was said while both tended to the meal. She asked, "Why do you want to move your law business here in, of all places, Virginia?"

"It's not for the money. I have more than I could ever spend in two lifetimes." He took a sip of his coffee then continued, "I'm tired of the constant limelight—well, mostly." He chuckled, "Seriously, my partner is expanding our law firm in California. And I really don't want the responsibility of training the newly hired lawyers to his way of thinking." The oven bell dinged.

Vivian checked the pasta, and while stirring, she asked, "So why have a business at all and why here?"

Jathrow eyes narrowed as he set the table and carried out the salad. Staying silent, he poured the orange drink, laced it with ice cream, and set the mint to the side.

Vivian loaded his plate with spaghetti and laid a baked chicken breast on top of the pasta, covering it with the graded cheese. Vivian sniffed. The cottage reeked with the home cooking they made. Silence continued between them except for the sound of silverware clattering.

It seemed forever before the dinner hour was over. The chairs scooted, and the dishes were cleared. They washed, dried, and placed them in the cabinet. Fresh coffee was brewed, and this time Jathrow poured each a cup of black coffee. Vivian brought blueberry muffins to the living room coffee table. Jathrow joined Vivian.

He cleared his throat. "Listen to me. I need to clear the air, and I want you to understand about the attorney's auction event night. I didn't stay with Nurse Betty in the way you must think. I discovered that Nurse Betty hadn't eaten before arriving at the event with Dr. Walter. She admitted she had one drink prior to dinner. Sadly after your doctor friend left with you, I was placed in an awkward situation. I didn't want the reporters or photographers to state anything harmful or negative about Nurse Betty or me or the fundraiser. And I was left alone with her. Viv, I escorted Nurse Betty to the diner on the outer edge of town where she drank coffee until three in the morning. I bought her breakfast and then called her a cab. I stayed at the diner a while longer, making a few phone calls before arriving at the cottage. It took me by surprise when you weren't home. No one let me in on why you left the event so suddenly. I was afraid something had happened to you."

Vivian opened her mouth, but Jathrow raised a hand. He paced assertively and said, "Not a word, woman! I need to say what I have to say." He took her hand. "The next morning, Richard Sr. and Ty both called me and asked if I would come in to Richard Sr.'s office. They ambushed and blamed me for you leaving the fund raiser without me." He locked heated eyes with Vivian. "I'm very disappointed you never gave me the benefit of the doubt. I've always been honest with you. You of all people should know how it is to be famous." He removed his hand from hers and crossed his chest. "It comes from one being powerful and successful. I thought you understood my position that night. At first, I only wanted you there as a front, but, Viv, I realized I only wanted to be there with you."

Vivian stirred, and moisture formed in her eyes. She dabbed her face and her shoulders began to shake. Jathrow lifted his hands and cradled Vivian. He rocked her back and forth. She snuggled in his safe, warm strength. He was all man. She cried harder. Hiccups returned, and Vivian watched Jathrow conceal his laughter. She punched his arm, and his muscles flexed. His blue eyes were beckoning, and the flecks were smoldering. Their breath mingled. She leaned in and touched his lips. Jathrow was not patient or gentle. He probed his tongue, enticing her lips to part. She edged her arms around him pulling his silken blond strands and whispered, "Jathrow."

He held her face in the palms of his hands and groaned. With a voice hardly audible, he uttered, "Vivian."

The kiss deepened, but a voice inside her warned, *Stop*. She pushed back, breathing unevenly, and blurted, "Jathrow, I think it's time for you to leave."

"Why? Why leave? Why can't we work things out?"

Vivian crossed her arms and rubbed them, struggling to gaining control. Finally she said, "I'm not a teenager anymore. I want you, Jathrow, that I know, but what I don't want from you is a one-night fling. So, mister, you need to keep trucking on down the road. Now!"

"But, Viv, I want there to be an…" He placed his hands on his hips and went silent. *What do I want to happen between us? Anything?* Jathrow, without hesitation, picked up his jacket, tossed it over his shoulder, and rushed out the cottage, shaking his head, letting the front door slam.

Vivian went to her desk, determined to write, but she pushed her writings to the floor, bowed her head in folded arms, and cried. *Wrong, I know, but I could have had the whole night with my…what? Friend, lover. Oh my, that was too close.*

Jathrow drove long into the night, blazing down the old country roads. However, he ran out of gas. He found himself sitting at a dead end. "Wouldn't you know, no OnStar and the bars on my cell phone are gone!" He hit the steering wheel. "What's wrong with me? I'm usually a calm man and know exactly what I want." Jathrow opened the car door, slid out, and walked to the trunk. Inside he found a survival kit consisting of a flashlight, can opener, can of red beans, blanket, and a sleeping bag. He shook the water jug; it was empty. He searched the grounds, and his foot touched a boulder. Jathrow threw his gear on the earth and built a campfire. He leaned against the rock, gazed at the stars and watched the dark clouds move in, covering the moon. The fire crackled, and he rubbed his hands over it. He stretched out on the sleeping bag and slipped off his shoes. The flame flickered and memories flashed back of a time when Vivian and his three friends, David, Ty, and Richard Sr. snuck away from their parents and so-called friends. The five personalities spent hours camping outdoors and talking about their future plans.

Jathrow chuckled and shook his head at remembering their great escapes. And then his buddies, David, Ty, and Richard Sr. never mention leaving Richmond, but they did talk at much length of future work plans and marriage.

He recalled sweet Vivian with her long red braided hair. How she would remain silent giving a nod now and then, but he would catch her glancing at him, and her soft green eyes held longing.

Jathrow stirred the fire and added twigs. With soul searching, he knew he had made the right decision in leaving Virginia in his youth. It was on the evening of his high school graduation, and he admitted it was hard leaving wide-eyed Vivian behind. He was unsettled in need to be with her, but once Jathrow arrived in California, he stored his juvenile feelings inside. He realized the thought of Vivian brought warm fuzziness to his being. Over the years, his feelings for her grew and had matured into a mind passion and a possessiveness of Vivian; however, he stayed distant. Was it love? Jathrow willed his thoughts and all-over-the-place emotions down and nodded.

He had fulfilled his must-have educational need and became both powerful and well-known. Money had been the key. Pride and confidence boosted when he obtained his life's goals. There never was a lack of women. He winced, recalling his first experience upon arriving in California.

Jathrow rubbed his burning eyes and needed sleep. Jathrow folded his suit coat under his head and decided when it was sunrise he would scout out his whereabouts. Now he waited for sleep to overcome him. Jathrow jolted as a drizzling drip hit his face. He stretched his eyes and saw the cloud of purple mingling with blackness. "It's rain." Jathrow prayed, "Lord, what's going on up there! Okay, so I'm ungrateful, well catty, and yes, sometimes vain, but really this?" He placed dirt over the fire. Then he picked up the half-rolled bed gear and threw it in the trunk. He sat on the boulder appearing more like an oversized drowned rat than a man who was tired and shivering. He prayed, "Almighty in space, I know You're real. What I don't understand is why, Lord, are You toying with me. Out of the million of people, You're picking on me."

Jathrow placed his hands over his eyes and tried to remember where he was located. *How am I going to get out of this?* He tried the car; it sputtered and then died. Jathrow was driven down on bended knees prayed, "Hello there. How do I begin? 'I'm sorry' seems so lame, but it's all I've got. I have the 'woe is me' attitude, like Elijah who ran from You, Lord. I'm alone, and I need Your help."

He opened his eyes; a sudden warm wind came, drying his clothes instantly. Some wrinkles appeared, but he had been protected and was provided for. A humming motor caught his ear. A truck was nearing. Jathrow waved his jacket and jumped up and down. It was David. Jathrow glanced to the sky and uttered a humble, "Thank You, Lord. I believe."

David scurried from the truck and socked Jathrow on the chin.

Ty jumped from the truck and pulled at David. After separating them, David addressed Jathrow. "You're a sorry source of a human being."

Jathrow rubbed his chin. Wide-eyed and with fists drawn, he said, "What's gotten into you?"

David, with fisted hands, screamed, "Vivian called me. She was crying, and she said, 'Look after Jathrow.' She refused to answer my call back. He took a step back and shook out his hands, then said, more calmly, "Chloe went over to the cottage to see if she could be of any help. In the mean time, Ty called me with a breakdown to his station wagon, and he needed a lift to a client's house." Finally David was able to joke, his anger had disappeared. "But my meeting was brief and the rain stopped. Along the way back I spotted your car," Ty inserted.

David said, "This is the area where we all camped in our teens. I knew you weren't at the hotel, for I had gone there first. On my way to pick up Ty, I called the realtor, and he hadn't seen you either. So why are you way out here?"

Jathrow kicked at the ground. "I needed to clear my head."

David huffed as he went to the truck and hauled a full can of gas to the car. He poured the gas into the tank, and Ty retrieved Jathrow's cell phone and plugged it into the truck's charger. David turned his eyes on Jathrow and said, "Vivian mentioned that the two of you quarreled. What's it all about?"

Jathrow with raised eyebrows answered, "If you must know, we are experiencing mix feelings and signals toward each other, although, yesterday, Vivian was the smart one, she stopped us before we made a horrible mistake." He hung his head and walked to the BMW. He cranked the motor, and it purred. He glanced at David, "I'm so confused. My body reacts willingly when it comes to Vivian, but my mind hesitates. I asked myself, do I want to commit? Is this love? Men, I won't string Vivian along."

Ty's soft voice injected, "If you are not interested in a life of forever with Vivian, then I suggest you let her go. She deserves much more."

Jathrow hunched his shoulders and said, "I have a lot of thinking to do. I'm stopping at the church."

David and Ty went silent and stared with open mouths. Jathrow paused at the car door and asked, "David, will you follow me to the gas station to make sure I get there?"

Ty walked over to Jathrow and handed back his cell phone. "Here, you have a couple of bars now."

12

The friends trailed each other. Jathrow stopped at the station and waved his friends on. Then he drove to a little white brick country church. There he slumped down in the front pew. He bowed his head and was surprised when his emotions oust, leaving him cry like a baby. "What is love?" *Vivian lights up my world, I care for her deeply, and my body wants her. Why couldn't we be comfortable with who we are?* "All right, Lord." He lifted his hands to the heavens. "I understand Your good book leaves instructions on marriage and the forever ball and chain. Here's my dilemma: marry Vivian, I can do, but love and the forever stuff—that's the real question. Will we get bored with each other and a hate set in? I'd die if we lost…us." Jathrow rose from the pew, shaking his head, and walked from the quaint church.

He slid behind the wheel and drove until he reached his new acquired building, pushing all thoughts of Vivian aside.

The realtor's SUV was parked in front, and he was pacing back and forth on the porch. He said, "I thought I must have missed you or I got our time wrong."

Jathrow shook hands and said, "I'm sorry I'm late."

The realtor handed over the key and led the way. As they were about to enter the building, David and Ty appeared. The four of them entered the building together.

David said, "This place has nice potential. What are you going to do with the loft rental?"

"Live here." Jathrow let out a sigh, then addressed Ty. "This place needs cleaned from top to bottom. Would you be interested in a permanent cleaning contract?" Not waiting for Ty to answer, Jathrow turned and placed an arm around David. "I'm needed in California ASAP to close up some loose ends. Would your schedule aid overseeing the architect, the decorating, hiring? I'm sure Richard Sr. will have references."

David nodded.

With wide arms, Jathrow said, "The front of the building needs to be all glass." Walking toward the loft, he said, "I want the loft sound proof."

David took notes, still nodding his head.

Jathrow continued down the hallway. "I want cherry wood throughout the building. And the receptionist desk to match."

David asked, "What about the floors in the conference rooms?"

Jathrow not batting an eye said, "Cream carpet." Jathrow kept walking and talking nonstop. "The loft needs to be modern, slick, and commercial-looking. You know with all stainless steel appliances and streamlined furniture."

David barked, "Helping with a project is one thing. But I do have a business to run!"

Jathrow paused. "I know this is going to require a lot of your time, and I know you are a hands-on person." Jathrow handed David a signed blank check. "That's why I need you." He smiled. "What I'm proposing is, this check will take care of the building and loft design plus all their furnishings." Jathrow scribbled his name on two other checks and handed one to David and said, "This is for all your trouble."

He walked over to Ty. "I know you're faithful, and you will not disappoint me in the cleaning. Here is some extra cash for cleaning supplies, and this check is for your services." Walking outside, Jathrow handed David the key and said, "See that Ty has a copy." He stepped a little further. "I would take care of this myself, but Mr. Stan Stout expects me back in the office tomorrow at seven o'clock." He turned to Ty. "Get what you need in cleaning materials, and I'll settle any differences with you when I get back. Just keep the bills, or call me." Jathrow's eyebrows arched. "Well, Ty?"

Ty had paled. "Here, take some of this money back. It's way too much!"

Jathrow chuckled, then said, "Do you want me to pay you less than I would someone else? This isn't because we are friends. Hiring you is a wise decision." Jathrow patted Ty on the back. "Besides, I trust you."

Jathrow walked to his car, and from the window, he said, "David, my law practice sign is ordered. It should arrive in a few weeks."

David with raised hand yelled, "How long will you be in California?"

"Hope no longer than three months. "I have my condo to sell. And I need to finish up the legal work for Mr. Stan Trout. My goal is to have all i's dotted and t's crossed and be back here soon."

David stepped closer to the vehicle and squatted. "Are you sure about settling here? Most folks in Virginia go to bed with the chickens, so to speak." He cleared his throat and continued. "Have you spoken with Vivian? And where do you stand with her?"

Jathrow lowered his car window more and rested his hands on the steering wheel. He locked eyes with David, "To both questions, no and no. I plan eventually on hiring attorneys that work cases are in different field from mine. And as talking with Vivian, well I need more time to think things out about an...us." A shallow smile crept on Jathrow's face. He drove toward the airport and didn't look back. Arriving there, he stored his vehicle in a pay/park zone and rushed inside to catch his California flight. Jathrow twisted and turned in his seat. He needed to table his thoughts on his future move to Virginia and his thoughts on Vivian and prepare himself for the present—his meeting with Mr. Stan Trout.

In the airport lobby, Stan Trout was pacing and holding a briefcase in hand. Jathrow waved, catching Stan's eye, and asked, "How are things?"

Mr. Stan Trout patted Jathrow's back. "Need you ask? It's hectic as always, but I wouldn't have it any other way."

Jathrow chucked, then replied, "How did the hospital accept Mr. Dan Neff in my stead to represent them? That position was long overdue to be filled. I definitely was out of my comfort zone. I know I am good, but my specialty is in divorce law."

Stan, not loosing gait, responded, "The position is not filled. I've set a meeting at the hospital for the two of you this afternoon at three o'clock. Here's the information you need to cinch the deal. I've asked Dan to shadow you over the next month or so."

"Stan, I don't like someone glancing over my shoulder. I work alone."

"Did I tell you Dan is interested in buying your condo?"

Jathrow's eyes widen. "Dan's ambitious enough. I sincerely hope he works out with the firm. What price did you quote him for the condo?"

"Full asking price! He didn't even bat an eye. Sort of reminds me of you when we first met."

They continued walking toward the waiting car when Jathrow turned and said, "Stan, I really do appreciate everything you made happen for me, but leaving all this behind will be sweet. Just letting you know I'm not going to miss this lifestyle at all."

❧❧

As the afternoon approached, Jathrow briefed Dan and moved through his business contacts. He assertively introduced Dan as his successor. Most management places and companies accepted Dan as Jathrow outwardly spoke appreciation of Dan

And in his confidence shown. However the claims department chose to continue with Jathrow until the end of the year. The medical health department and musical staff went with Dan and stayed with Stan's firm. Large and private firms spoke of their torn thoughts of Jathrow's decision of practicing law in his own hometown. However, all agreed he would still be credited with helping businesses achieved in California.

Within several months, both Jathrow and Stan stood shaking hands in the courtroom after the judge made his final ruling, dissolving the longstanding partnership's law practice. Stan Trout now owned his standalone firm, and Jathrow Mowey now owned his. They hugged and clapped each other on the back, knowing at least their law business was happily dissolved and their friendship was kept in tact.

Jathrow stayed at the condo another month until Dan raised the hefty amount one million point two thousand dollars and paid for the condo. Title exchanged.

Exactly fifteen days later, a newspaper journalist/photographer had a field day interviewing Jathrow, and he wrote, "Jathrow Mowey leaving California and seeking private practice in Virginia. Is there an exclusive woman in the wings in hopes of catching the world's most eligible bachelor?" Jathrow laughed at the pathetic press. A woman waiting for him, what a laugh.

He hailed a cab and sighed. *I haven't heard from Vivian or her daughter in a very long time.* He rubbed his chin at the airport and sent a text to David: "See you soon!" His flight was exhausting although it only lasted a few hours. He paid the parking fee and drove the red BMW to his new law office building.

Jathrow stood in front, trying to think where David might have left the key. He fished in the mailbox, and there it was; only now there were two different sets of keys. He checked his watched and reset the time for the watch showed a three-hour difference from California.

The sun had lost its pinkness in the horizon. And the one-eighth quarter moon had risen. It was almost pitch black, and the hour was late. Jathrow took a deep breath, saying, "I'm glad to be home, Virginia." He glanced at the huge sign and rocked back and forth with admiration. "What a beauty." He fingered the sculptured front window, admiring the steel frames. He all but danced with happiness.

Jathrow unlocked the front door and stepped inside. He enjoyed the heavenly smell of wood as an overhead light automatically came on and brightened the lobby. Jathrow gasped at the lustrous beauty of the receptionist desk and ran his hand over it. He had bounce in his steps as he entered his office and visited the warm colors and inviting seating arrangements. He was not disappointed when he saw the conference rooms in all their grandeur. Matching chandeliers hung with their magnificent glitter. The wall art was exceptional, all top class. His chest puffed out, thinking how his friend David had devoted his time in making this building an art display. David spared no expense.

Jathrow stepped outside the building to lock up. From out of nowhere, red and blue lights flashed through the air. A police officer yelled, "Stand still. Put your hands behind your head and spread your feet."

Jathrow willed his throbbing heart to regulate its beating. He opened his mouth, wanting to speak, but the officer held a stun gun. He heard another voice and was glad to see David. He breathed a long sigh of relief.

David said, "Hello, Officer Patrick Daily. I'm sorry about all this." David swung his arms and continued, "I just checked my phone and saw that Jathrow was arriving tonight. He beat me here. I was about to free the alarm."

Jathrow paled. He hadn't even thought about an alarm.

He spoke, "I'm sorry, Officer." He winced when he looked over at David.

David said, "Officer Daily has your building on his route."

Jathrow reddened and said, "Again, I'm sorry, sir, for my laxity. I didn't know about an alarm. My fault."

The officer moved aside and said, "Mr. Jathrow Mowey, you may put your hands down now." A chuckle escaped. "Welcome to the community. I've heard about you!"

Jathrow nodded as he watched the police car disappear.

"Is there a separate alarm for the apartment?"

David nodded and grabbed Jathrow in a bear hug. He later showed Jathrow the private entrance the architect created for accessing the loft. David punched in the code number and explained, "The key entry for the loft is 514 and your business is 415."

"What?"

David slid Jathrow a card containing the key codes, which were highlighted. He replied, "For the apartment, I use the number 5 as in five friends. The number 1 represents the one that left, and the number 4 stands for how many friends stayed behind, hence 514. However, your business key code is reversed. Beginning with 4 friends who remained, for 1 who left, but then returned, thus making 5."

Jathrow sniffled, adjusted his shoulders, then slapped David on the back. "You sentimental old friend, but thank you in the way you think!"

The men stepped inside the loft, and Jathrow's mouth gaped. "Wow! Would you look at the view? It's breathtaking. I can see the skyline all the way downtown with the mountains behind." Jathrow was moved, and tears lurked in his eyes. Shifting again, he said, "David, this is outstanding. The amount of concrete and steel used, you're a man after my own heart. And can you believe the furniture! It's retro! Where did you find everything? I'm very impressed. You even captured the color scheme—black, white, and a splash of red. It's to die for. How much extra do I owe you?"

David's jaw dropped. "I have money left over." And bit his lip. "After all, you allowed me to spend a lot of zeros."

"Man, I didn't pay you enough." Jathrow whipped out his checkbook and scribbled a few figures, shoved the check into David's hand, and said, "I won't take no for an answer."

As the men walked outside, Jathrow stopped. He placed his hands on his hips. "Did Ty buy the new truck he was admiring before I left?"

David kicked at an imaginary pebble. "No. Lots of things happened in Ty's life although it never stopped him from coming to work. Overall, he only missed two days of work, and that was when his wife was hospitalized." David shook his head and continued, "Lillian took a spell, but is home now but is required to have a nurse 24-7. So his money again is spoken for."

Jathrow shook his head. "Ty is such a nice guy. He deserves better." He looked at David. "How long will Lillian need a nurse?"

David shrugged his shoulders. "I'm not sure she will ever be without a nurse. The specialist discovered Lillian has a bone degenerative disease."

Jathrow blew a low whistle. "How sad. I'm sure Ty has accepted this and is trusting in God, but I think I can help. David, mum is the word." Jathrow turned, flipping open his cell phone and punched in a number. "Hello, Stan. Yes, I know what time it is, and yes, I'm fine. I arrived a little while ago. Listen. I need a huge favor, so please call it in. Hold on then, I will give you all the details." Jathrow looked at David and rolled his eyes. He walked with David to the truck and once again thanked him for all the work and his help. Jathrow held the cell phone out and mouthed, "David, I need to talk with you later…about a friend of ours."

David nodded. "I'll call tomorrow. You really do have a heart."

Jathrow took the stairs two at time to his loft and said, "Thanks for holding, Stan. Now here's the plan. Call Mr. John Glitching and let him know I'm calling in a favor. And since he is your business associate, he said all I needed to do was ask. I want a white Ford panel truck. The top of the line. And it needs to be loaded with commercial and home cleaning equipment as well as the cleaning solutions. Everything that's available. The truck is to be delivered to Mr. Ty Sow. Take down the address. Under no circumstance is Ty to know that the truck came from me. Promise?"

13

Jathrow was up to his eyeballs with customers. His law firm had been opened for ten days, and he realized an urgent need to hire more attorneys and a receptionist. In between clients, he wrote and placed an ad with the state's newspaper asking all attorneys interested in a full-time position to stop in his building by ten o'clock the next day. He called an employment agency in hopes of finding a suitable receptionist for his law practice but was instantly informed, "The agency has no one available."

Jathrow arrived in his office at 8:30 a.m. and was lost in his work when his office was rushed with twenty-five eager lawyers seeking work. He rose, lifting his hands, and said, "Thank you all for coming. Follow me in to the west conference room." He passed out an hour-long test and pencils to each person, instructing them, "No help. You're on your own!" He set the timer and walked from the room.

The front door bell dinged. The phones were ringing off the hook. He saw a shadow of a woman and just said, "Just take a seat at the desk and please answer the phone. If anyone wants to speak with me, directly take a name and number. I'm not available." He popped his head out in the hallway, adding, "We'll discuss pay later, and I'll make it up to you. Thanks." He closed his office door and checked the time.

The hour passed quickly, and he gathered the tests. He bid all a farewell and thanked them for coming out. He said, "I'll call by ten o'clock tomorrow morning for the applicants I've selected. And, again, thanks for your time."

Jathrow tapped his desk as he carefully reviewed the test and was surprised that only two had qualified. Jathrow decided not to wait and called the two possibilities. He presented his proposal to each man and asked they take twenty-four hours before they accept or decline his offer, and he demanded their discretion. He also penned a projective time on the calendar for their appointments. He wondered if either man would show. He expected a lot, and after all, they would be paid an outlandish salary.

The bell dinged, and it was already 3:30 p.m. He again heard familiar voices talking. Jathrow stepped into the foyer with his shirtsleeves rolled under and a loose fitting silk tie. He viewed Vivian speaking with Ty. His eyes widened. "Did you both come in together?" Jathrow looked over at the desk. "Now where did the receptionist disappear to?" Jathrow broke into a smile and placed his hands on his narrow hips. "It's sure nice to see you both. How can I help?"

Ty reached for Jathrow and gave him a friendly hug and spoke, "Do you know anything about a white panel truck? I received a strange call. A dealership called me saying they had a customized, fully loaded commercial cleaning truck paid for and needed it delivered. You're the only one I know with that kind of money." He jumped up and down and waved his hand in the air. "I picked up the truck and left him my old station wagon." He laughed.

Jathrow glanced around, still not seeing the receptionist. "Do you have time to show me your new truck?"

The excitement exploded in Ty as he all but hopped outside, admiring his new Ford truck.

"It's awesome." Then he patted Ty on the back. "Friend, you did an outstanding job cleaning both building and loft. So am I on your route full-time?"

There was no hesitation on Ty's part. He yelled, "When do you want me?"

Jathrow threw his head back, laughing. "Is tomorrow too soon?"

Ty interrupted, "Tomorrow seven o'clock I'll be here." He tipped his hat at Vivian and then slid behind the wheel of his shiny new truck. He sounded the horn and waved. "See you tomorrow, Jathrow, and thank you."

Jathrow noticed Vivian hadn't moved, and she appeared speechless. "What, Vivian?"

She said, "I came to your office early this morning. I wanted to welcome you back to Virginia and take a tour of your new building. However, I made out a bill for my services rendered and placed it in your mail slot."

Jathrow's blue eyes bulged as she giggled, walking toward her car. "Whatever do you mean, Vivian? A bill for what?"

Her smile crept reaching the corner of her green eyes, and softness appeared on her face. "Got ya! I was the receptionist today." Shaking her head, she breathed, "You really didn't know, did you?"

Jathrow croaked a weak "No." He walked to where she stood. "Would you care for your tour now?"

Not waiting for an answer, he touched Vivian's elbow and guided her through the glass doors and down the main building hallway.

Vivian made small talk while stopping to finger the hung paintings. She ran her hand on the tabletop and touched the draperies. Ever so quietly, she said, "It's hard to believe this grand building is not located in New York." She glanced at the clock and announced, "Oh my, would you look at the time. It's past five! Sorry, Jathrow, but I have a dinner engagement." Over her shoulder, she said, "With Sam. Bye, friend."

With his jaw dropped, Jathrow watched her all but waltz to her new magnificent sports car. "Where's the Vivian I used to know? So sweet, down to earth, wearing floppy hats. Now she's more confident, independent, and skinny, dressed in ritzy clothes."

The office phone rang, catching Jathrow's attention. He had to hurry. "Hello, this is Jathrow Mowery, attorney-at-law. How may I help you?"

"Well, well, well, Jathrow, this is Richard Sr. Pair. I've called to see if the position for a receptionist has been filled?"

"You applying?" Jathrow stretched his head from side to side, then said, "No, the position is still open. Hey, Richard Sr., can you meet me at the old diner outside town?"

In his baritone voice Richard Sr. scuffed, "Give me an hour, and I'll be there. Jathrow?"

"It will be great seeing you. Yes, Richard Sr.?"

"Welcome back, friend."

"Thanks. See you in an hour."

Long after the phone was hung up, Jathrow sat at the receptionist's desk with his head leaned back. His mind could not shake the beautiful image Vivian had left trailing behind. Jathrow glanced at the decorative hand-carved clock and shoved from the chair, hurrying to his loft, and showered. He flew down the back roads in a flurry, heading toward the diner. He was surprised to fine Richard Sr. had not arrived, but Richard

Sr. was always running late. Jathrow's stomach growled, so he entered the diner. A waitress, who wore a way-too-small tank top, led him to a table. She breathed over his shoulder while popping her gum. In a husky voice, she leaned in and asked, "What would you like tonight?" She raised an eyebrow and batted her brown eyes. "See anything on the menu?" She licked her lips and added, "Or ala carte?"

His eyes narrowed, and he glanced toward the door. Jathrow stood and almost knocked the waitress over as he reached for Richard Sr.'s hand to shake. "I'm glad you're here."

The waitress, still chewing her gum, pointed, "So, big man, are you joining him?"

Her eyes gave Richard Sr. the once-over, and they swiftly returned back to Jathrow, and her smile broadened. Richard Sr. disregarded the waitress and slapped Jathrow on the back. He straddled the chair and voiced, "It's so nice having you back home. I'm glad you decided to open your firm here. How's the office?"

The waitress cleared her throat and kept tapping her pad. "Well, are you men ordering or not?"

Jathrow asked for another menu and held up his cup. The waitress popped her gum again, poured the coffee, and stomped from the table. Jathrow shook his head, saying, "I should have made the move years ago." He sipped his coffee and asked, " Have you seen my establishment? You know, David did an outstanding job for me. Both the loft and law building are wickedly sweet. I also can't leave out good ole Ty, for he certainly handled the entire daily cleaning needs. He's very efficient. That's why I hired him on permanently."

Richard Sr. sipped his coffee. "I had the privilege of being at your building site and was able to watch the men insert the large glass windows. David invited me in, and I was amazed at the finishes and the floors. I didn't get to see your loft though, but I've heard. It's every single man's dream." Richard Sr. stood and whistled for the waitress. Both men ordered country steak with whipped potatoes and a side serving of green beans. After they finished dinner, the waitress gathered the dirty dishes and popped her gum. "How about warm apple pie with a dip of vanilla ice cream?"

Richard Sr. patted his barrel stomach and answered, "Why not."

Jathrow held up his cup for another refill of coffee. His smile disappeared when he inquired, "Is there something going on between Vivian and Mr. Samuel Gee?"

Richard Sr. set his cup down hard and then answered, "It's none of my business, but since you've asked, Vivian did confide in me, saying you never indicated to her if you wanted more than friendship with her. So she's moving on with her life."

Jathrow leaned forward, speaking in a low whisper, "Is it serious between them?"

Richard Sr. stroked his stubbly chin. "Honestly, Jathrow, Mr. Samuel Gee would marry Vivian tomorrow if she would only say yes. He gave her a ring. And it's still in the box. But I do think she is considering his offer though."

Jathrow breathed deep and slowly released, then said, "I came back to Virginia to be near Vivian. I had hoped we might date and see where it could lead, but Vivian seems to want more than a surfer man." Jathrow poked his now pathetic-looking piece of pie. " What does Vivian want?" Jathrow raised a hand as if pleading a case, then added, "She's been married before, has a daughter, and is successful in her own rights. So again, what does the woman want?"

Richard Sr. stood up. He glared down at Jathrow, and his beady gray eyes narrowed. He barked, "Friend, have you ever considered settling down? You know, like marriage, only to one woman!"

Jathrow held his cup in midair, mouth open. He pointed to himself and screeched, "Me marry?" His blue eyes widened. Sputtering, he said, "I thought at first, Vivian just wanted to be on old friendlier terms. But since we are not perusing a one-night…"

"I guess you were wrong. And when did our Vivian ever fool around?"

Jathrow tossed a roll of money on the table, stood, and walked out of the restaurant, leaving Richard Sr. standing in silence. At their vehicles, Richard Sr. thundered, "Vivian is a church-going, God-fearing woman. After she met Doc, she went to church faithfully and has attended ever since, unless she's out of town." Richard Sr. shut his car door and zoomed from the lot.

Jathrow realized he hadn't spoken with Richard Sr. about a receptionist, and he decided against calling him. Several evenings later, he called Stan in LA and asked if he knew of a reliable woman with secretarial/

receptionist skills who would want to relocate. He was happily surprised when Stan furnished him with a name. Jathrow called after giving Stan time to contact her. When Jathrow called, a pleasant voice answered the line. "Hello. This is Jathrow Mowey. Is this Sandra Hills?"

There was hesitation, and then a pure sweetness filled the air. "This is Sandra Hills. I was expecting your call, Mr. Mowey."

Jathrow let out a long breath and said, "Thank you in advance for your directness. The position available is for a receptionist and a personal secretary in one. Would you be interested in a one-month trial? All expenses would be paid by me if you and I come to an agreement."

"I am. Would this be full-time employment should this work out?""

"It is. Ms. Hills, would you fax me your résumé?"

"Sir, I'm sending one your way right now. What's the fax number?"

There was a click and buzz. He then received Sandra's résumé and glanced over it while nodding his head. He asked, "Ms. Hills, what income and benefits are you expecting? How fast can you get here?"

"Let me think." There was a tapping from a pen across the line. "Mr. Mowey, I can arrive the first of the week. Is there a boarding house in town?"

"I'll take care of your arrangements. And thank you for your promptness. I will need your word on complete confidentiality in all matters."

"Mr. Mowey, I'm surprised you felt the need to say anything. I'm honorable and reliable."

"Your impeccable reputation precedes you from Stan. However, I just wanted all t's crossed and all i's dotted. I'll expect to see you on Monday. Let's say 8:30 a.m." He hung up. Jathrow thought, *Ms. Hills would be a great asset to my law business.* Glancing at her résumé again, he studied Ms. Sandra Hill's picture and recalled she had been married to a judge he had appeared in front of many times. He wondered out loud, "Is she still married?" Jathrow made a note to call Stan.

He locked up the law building and went upstairs. Jathrow changed into his running gear and went for a long jog. The brisk air tousled his long blond hair. He tried sorting through the confusion in his personal life. He asked himself, *Does Vivian fit into my plans?* He shook his head and pushed further running.

A few months passed, the law business kept growing. The newly hired attorneys proved their worth. Jathrow personally praised Sandra Hills for being such a godsend and complimented her perfection. He appreciated her strict dress code. Jathrow remembered the very first day Ms. Hills arrived. It made him laugh.

That Monday, she arrived one hour earlier than scheduled. She hurried through the front door and collided with him. Ms. Hills set her purse down along with two suitcases. She adjusted her pillbox hat, and with hands on hips, she said, "Mr. Mowey, I'm sure Stan has relayed to you that I am single. My late husband, Judge Peterson, died recently. And, sir, may I speak frankly."

Jathrow's lips uplifted as he motioned her to sit. Jathrow remained standing. "Don't stop now."

She twisted her hands in her lap, saying, "Sir, you are a handsome man, as you know. But let's keep our relationship professional."

"I'm sure we're on the same page, Ms. Hills." He breathed, then said, "And for the record, I'm interested in someone."

She nodded.

His voice trailed as he lifted his arms. "But it seems to be a one-way street, which is not open for discussion, not now, not ever!"

Ms. Hills rose and pointed to her luggage. She reached for her purse and marched to the massive receptionist desk where she plumped down and powered up the computer. Jathrow mumbled to himself as he removed Ms. Hills's luggage. A few hours later, he presented Ms. Hills with her room key, location, and gave her the house rules and information.

A few evenings later, Jathrow escorted Ms. Hills to dinner with intentions of discussing a private business matter. However, they were followed, and a camera crew caught a glimpse of the new woman seated with Jathrow and horned in. Pictures were taken. Jathrow began to rise, but Ms. Hills covered his hand and smiled directly at the camera. He sighed, knowing the press would once again rumor about his bachelorhood. He also knew the news of a mystery woman would generate more business in his law practice. Jathrow basked in the spotlight and gave in to the moment of interest. As they were sipping coffee after dinner, Ms. Sandra Hills said, "I know the topic of the woman you pine for is taboo, but have you heard from her?"

Jathrow frowned as he shook his head. "She's seeing someone else."

"Well," Sandra patted his hand. "Is it serious?"

The camera folk snapped another photo.

Jathrow stared into Ms. Hills's huge brown eyes. "I don't know." He then stood and helped Sandra from her chair. As he glanced at her, it was as if he were seeing Ms. Hills for first time. She wore a royal blue strapless form fitting evening dress with a flare behind the knee. With her stylish midnight raven hair, she was quite beautiful. Walking from the restaurant, they stopped and posed again for the camera.

Jathrow still had doubts about Vivian and what his true feelings were; in fact, he was miserable. A few days later, he e-mailed Ms. Sandra Hills to send flowers and pink roses to Vivian along with a "thinking of you" card. His business had him flying from Virginia to California. He checked in daily with Ms. Hills, and she forwarded notes, contracts, business forms, or any other information needed. But when evening came, he knew only loneliness and emptiness. He had sworn off from all women. Jathrow felt drained and carried a restless soul.

Ms. Sandra Hills called while he was out. He listened to the voice message and hit four for replay.

"Vivian's agent Samuel Gee called the law office and wanted to know if Jathrow Mowery would be attending Vivian's after-five dinner party on Friday. Also would he be bringing a date? How do you wish me to reply? Call me!"

His stomach rolled. Jathrow raked his hands through his hair. *What to do?* He decided to call David, knowing he would be catering the party. On the third ring, David answered, "Hello, David's Catering. How may I help you?"

"Hello, David, this is Jathrow. Are you catering Vivian's shindig on Friday?"

David's baritone voice bustled though the air. "It's good to hear from you. And to answer your question, yes, I'm catering. Did you want to know the menu?"

Jathrow sighed. "No. But what's the occasion?" Then he sucked in air. "Friend, is Vivian engaged?"

"For someone with your confidence in the law practice field, you sure are a mouse when it comes to your personal life." David blew out air, then said, "You are on your own this time about Vivian. I'm staying clear of your personal life. I'm catering. Good night, Jathrow!"

Jathrow held the silent phone, then slammed it down. He took a cold shower and still wasn't at peace. He picked up his new law file, and the words all ran together. He flipped on the TV and found only home improvement shows. Jathrow paced the floors but stubbed his toe. He hobbled while rubbing his big toe and realized it was Friday in the wee hours, and he hadn't replied to Mr. Samuel Gee's invitation. He reached for his cell phone and called Ms. Sandra Hills. The phone kept on ringing, and he was ready to hang up when Sandra answered, "Mr. Mowery, what on earth is wrong?"

"Nothing...*everything*, Ms. Hills."

"Well, our time is three hours difference, so?"

He rushed, "I've decided to attend Vivian's dinner party, and I need a date for superficial purposes. Can you arrange this on such short notice?"

Time passed before Sandra sighed and replied, "Do tell, Jathrow, it's three o'clock in the morning. And for your information, you are confirmed with a date to Vivian's dinner party. Only your date select fell ill, so I am pitching in for her, but hear me out, don't get any wrong ideas. This is business only!"

"Thanks, Ms. Hills, and I understand loud and clear. You're a lifesaver. I'll send you flowers."

"Jathrow, listen, there's no need to send flowers. They have already been sent. We'll talk later. I'm going back to sleep. Good night and good-bye."

Jathrow glanced in the mirror and saw he was wearing a stupid grin. He padded back to bed, turned on his side, and pulled up the sheet. He could still feel the smile on his face when he awoke an hour later. Jathrow was on the 5:00 a.m. flight, which landed in Virginia on time. A short while later, he presented the scheduled pressing day of negotiations in his office. He noted that one couple decided to seek counsel; another couple argued, not mincing words seeking a divorce; while another young married couple decided on dissolution. By the end of the day, Jathrow usually felt beaten up from people's life situations, but today was different. In a few short hours, he would see Vivian. He motioned Ms. Hills into his office. "Do we know why Vivian is throwing a party?"

She twisted her mouth and answered, "No." Ms. Hills paused a moment, then said, "I need to leave, and I need you to be at the rooming house on the porch promptly by six." She backed from his office, closing the door. It was after four when Jathrow's receptionist/secretary left work. He placed the Close sign on the door and locked up the building. He headed to his loft to prepare for the evening's black-tie event.

14

Jathrow parked his sports car in front of the boarding house. He checked his Rolex: 5:55 p.m. Ms. Hills was waiting on the porch. He tipped his hat and handed her a bouquet of violets. His blue eyes danced, seeing the different shades reflecting from Ms. Hills purple dress. The corners of Jathrow's mouth lifted as he gave his receptionist the look. "Sinful." Jathrow kissed her cheek and offered her his arm. He seated Ms. Hills in his prized red Roadster and walked to his side of the car. He placed his hand on the down button when Ms. Hills waved a finger glove at him, saying, "Leave the top up."

They arrived at the cottage. Ms. Hills clutched Jathrow's elbow. The door swung wide, and Mr. Gee stepped forward rocking back and forth on the balls of his feet. He stopped moving as his green eyes ogled the woman at Jathrow's side. Jathrow's smile deepened, knowing the effect Ms. Hills had on men. Her dress plunged both front and back, and the sides were cut in small diamond shapes, giving peek-a-boo effect. Jathrow thought if it weren't for the length, there wouldn't be much of a dress.

Ms. Hills nudged Jathrow. He winked and said, "Mr. Samuel Gee, meet Ms. Sandra Hills. And Ms. Hills, this is Mr. Samuel Gee." Jathrow rubbed his hands together and asked, "Mind if we come in?"

Ms. Hills removed her glove and smiled. Her hand extended. Mr. Gee's eyes twinkled and widened. He reached for her hand and kissed it. He said, his eyes not leaving Ms. Hills, "Jathrow, you know almost everyone here. Why don't you go ahead and mingle."

Mr. Gee stepped back and offered his arm to Ms. Hills.

Jathrow's eyebrows shot up, and as he was about to speak, Ms. Hills nodded. Jathrow adjusted his shoulders and stepped inside alone.

Mr. Gee asked, "Ms. Hills, would you care for a glass of punch or something to eat?"

Jathrow smothered a laugh as he walked greeting men and women in the room. A duet began. Jathrow leaned on the doorframe, crossed his arms, and listened. His neck hair rose, and he knew who was near. Jathrow pivoted and was face-to-face with Vivian. He ran a finger around the neck of his shirt. He couldn't breath. Her red hair had blond highlights, which waved across her shoulders. The little black dress molded to her curves. His heart beat faster. As he breathed, her perfume wavered under his nose. Jathrow stepped forward and kissed Vivian's cheek. He chanced a look; she was smiling. Then she abruptly said, "Where's your lady friend?"

Jathrow remembered Ms. Hills. He jerked his head searching through the crowd and answered, "Ms. Hills is with your Mr. Gee. And I see they are heading our way."

Vivian turned when Ms. Hills approached. "Hello, Mrs. Rose. It's nice to be here tonight. Ah, and the couple's duet was lovely." Ms. Hills glanced at Mr. Gee, patted his arm, and then continued, "Mr. Gee has informed me there is more entertainment to come. I'm looking forward to the evening." Ms. Hills reached for Jathrow's hand and batted her brown eyes. He narrowed his baby blues and raised his brows. He leaned in to Ms. Hills and whispered, "What's going on?"

Ms. Hills nudged Jathrow toward the garden. With hands on her slender hips, she said, "Jathrow, help me out!"

He tilted his head and whispered, "Help you how?"

She bit her lip. "I want to pursue Mr. Gee. I think he's really hot!"

"What?"

Vivian materialized in the garden, joining Ms. Hills and Jathrow. He straightened and said, "It's lovely out here."

Ms. Hills excused herself and left the garden.

Vivian asked, "Would you walk with me on the beach?"

Jathrow's thoughts weren't on walking; he wanted to take her in his arms. But the plea of Ms. Hills asking him for help nagged him. He looked down at Vivian's ring finger and into her eyes. Vivian's smile faded. She walked away and over her shoulder murmured, "Maybe some other time."

Jathrow's heart hit his stomach. Mr. Gee waved and caught up with Vivian. He announced, "It's time to let everyone in on the surprise!"

Vivian turned, patting Samuel's arm. "So it is." As an afterthought, she asked, "Coming, Jathrow?"

He forced a smile and answered, "I'm right behind you." He walked through the door and joined the crowd now gathered around the stage. Ms. Hills touched his waist. On tiptoe, she asked, "What's going on?"

Jathrow rubbed his hands and swallowed. Looking down at Ms. Sandra Hills, he flared, "Don't know."

Mr. Gee was on stage and motioned for Vivian Rose.

The room quieted as she was handed a mic. She said, "Testing, one, two, three." The mic screeched, and the people laughed. She cleared her throat and began again. "Hello, everyone, I hope you're getting plenty to eat. If not, blame David Fleck."

The room hooted. Vivian continued, "The entertainment is provided by Ty Sow." She paused, allowing the clapping crowd to quiet. Vivian folded her hands and said, "Will Richard Jr. and Jacey please join me on stage."

The audience cheered. Jacey rubbed her stomach.

Jathrow's eyes widened. Her face was round, and her feet were like balloons. "Jacey is pregnant."

Richard Jr.'s arms were only partly around Jacey. He was beaming. Richard Jr. dropped his arm and reached for Jacey's enlarged pudgy hand, saying, "We're married. We intended to have a formal wedding here in Virginia, but the stork found us in Las Vegas, where we married."

The room hooted and raved. The band struck a cord. The crowd hollered again. Jathrow let out a breath. He heard his name. Jacey was motioning for Jathrow to go up. He mustered a smile and stepped forward, kissing her cheek, then shook hands with Richard Jr. He congratulated them both on their marriage and their upcoming baby. He turned, catching Vivian's sparkling green eyes, and from nowhere, he said, "How about me hosting the baby shower?" Vivian rushed to Jathrow's side, and seconds later, Mr. Gee joined them. He opened his arms and said, "Baby shower is on."

Mr. Gee asked, "What is needed for the baby?"

Jacey giggled and replied, "Everything. We're having triplets!"

Jathrow walked over to Jacey stopping just shy of a blushing Vivian. He asked, "Jacey, when would you like the shower?"

Ms. Hills drew her cell phone from her purse and thumped the calendar. She waved, catching Jathrow's attention. He stepped forward and stopped, "What?"

She whispered in his ear, "Your calendar is clear Friday, September 5, or on the October 7."

He nodded and rejoined Vivian. He said, "Here are the dates available."

Vivian talked with Jacey and then announced, "The baby shower will be at Jathrow's building this Friday. Although quick notice, please be sure and take note." She blushed again.

All left the stage. Ms. Hills joined Vivian and Jacey. They all talked at once, sounding like swarming bees or clucking chickens. Jathrow shook his head and walked outside. Richard Sr. and his son joined Jathrow, as well as Mr. Gee. Jathrow pulled his jacket collar up and rubbed his hands. Richard Sr. nodded and slapped Jathrow on the back and said, "Thanks, friend, for stepping forward for the kids."

Jathrow hunched his shoulders and said, "It seemed like the right thing to do." He chuckled. "I'll only be paying the bill. You know, the ladies will be all over the party." He glanced at Richard Jr. "Young man, get in the habit of carrying your checkbook and being a yes-man."

Richard Sr. chuckled, nodded, and patted Jathrow on the back. "You can say that again. I learned my lesson a long time ago."

Mr. Gee said, "Jathrow, thanks for taking the lead about the shower. See you this Friday at three o'clock."

Jathrow scrolling watched as Mr. Gee stalked towards his car, and questioned, "Does Vivian really have romantic feelings for Mr. Gee?" Jathrow and the other men went back inside the house. Ms. Hills was waiting. "Hello, gentlemen." She smiled and tugged at Jathrow's jacket. He twisted and waved to the men. When they were out of earshot he said, "What?"

She whispered, "Walk with me."

He nodded and placed her hand over his and began to walk. Outside, Ms. Hills drew her hand away from Jathrow and waved to Mr. Gee, who was standing by his sedan. Jathrow hunched his shoulders, waiting. Ms. Hills said, "I need you to leave the party now."

"Why, Ms. Hills?" She continued walking, and Jathrow followed. Mr. Gee opened the passenger door and motioned for Ms. Hills to slide in. Mr. Gee took quick steps to the other side of the car and fumbled with his keys. Jathrow, docile as a lamb, pulled ahead of Mr. Gee's car and drove to the office. He unlocked the door and punched in the alarm code, disarming it. Ms. Hills and Mr. Gee walked in behind Jathrow; Mr. Gee winked and walked toward the west conference room, holding Ms. Hills's hand.

Ms. Hills said, "We want to be alone and talk."

Jathrow nodded "Lock up when you're done in here, Ms. Hill. I'll be upstairs if you need me."

Jathrow keyed in the code, set the alarm, and left the law building. He climbed the stairs to his flat. Jathrow stripped from his clothes, wearing just briefs, and sprawled in a chair. He turned on the TV and flipped through the channels where he found his favorite classic movie, *Casablanca.* Jathrow recalled when all five friends sat through the movie. It also was Vivian's favorite. He pushed up from the chair and made buttery popcorn .

After the movie, Jathrow carried the bowl to the kitchen's sink. He opened the refrigerator and took a bottled water. He padded to the bed and propped himself, leaving all the decorative pillows on the bed. Jathrow sipped the water and yawned but wasn't sleepy. He reached for the Bible and read Psalms 23 where he usually found peace. He shivered, realizing the heat hadn't come on; however, he refused to turn up the thermostat. He muttered as he pulled on his jeans. *I'll just grab a novel and read.* Stepping over to the wall of library books, he fingered Vivian's novels.

The doorbell dinged. He glanced at the time. It was 10:30 p.m. Thinking it was Ms. Sandra Hills, he flung open the door. His jaw dropped. "Vivian?"

She pointed to his chest and said, "Well, are you going to show me your place or not?" Vivian had decided to take matters in her own hands and confront Jathrow searching out his feelings toward her. She had a drink of bubbly earlier and felt bold. Her green eyes widened.

Jathrow backed up, and his heart thumped really fast as she stepped inside. She slid off her wrap. He gulped, seeing that she was still in that little black dress. "Um…I'll be right back." He returned in a shirt not yet completely buttoned. He coughed and asked, "Why stop by tonight, Vivian?"

She touched his lips with her fingers and said, "I wanted to personally thank you for volunteering for Jacey and Richard Jr.'s baby shower."

Jathrow inhaled while looking away. On tiptoe, Vivian nibbled at his earlobe. Cocking his head, he breathed, "Whoa, Viv." He backed up, adding, "You're treading on dangerous territory here."

Her lips touched his perfectly shaped lips, and her hand slid to his bare chest. Vivian whispered, "And?"

Jathrow placed both his hands on her sweetheart shoulders, and the room spun. Suddenly his three-thousand-square-foot loft seemed more like a matchbox. After a step backward, he said, "Um, come let me show you around." He began to button up his shirt.

Vivian blurted, "Are you and Ms. Hills an item?"

Jathrow sucked in air, calming his raspy breathing. "No! Sandra—er, Ms. Hills has never been an interest of mine." His blue flickering eyes narrowed, and his voice quivered, "Viv, it's always been you.But I heard you and Mr. Gee have interest in each other. Am I wrong?"

She ran her hands through his long locks, tilted her head, and breathed, "Oh Jathrow, what are we going to do?"

Jathrow clutched the rail by the loft's wall of windows facing the city. His heart was racing. He wondered if she could hear his heart beating. He moaned, "I'll show you around my place some other time, but for now, I'm protecting your reputation." He reached for her hand and walked.

Vivian pouted. "Where are we going?"

He remained silent and guided her downstairs. Jathrow saw that Samuel's car was gone. He let out a sigh.

"I'll follow you home where we can take that walk on the beach."

Vivian laughed and reached for her keys. She strummed a finger down his chest and said, "Jacey is staying at the cottage. Richard Jr. bought a house, and it's being remolded. He's adding room for the nanny. Jacey will need all the help she can get with triplets. Last report from the architect was to expect another week before move in ready." Vivian glanced into Jathrow's large blue eyes, and using her index finger, she traced his full mouth and lowly said, "See you soon?"

Jathrow stood barefoot hardly breathing, watching Vivian's taillights disappear. *What just happened here?* He sat on the ground , not caring how cold it was. He willed down his surprise. *Did Vivian want more from me? Was she personally free from her agent? Or had she been teasing?* He was confused and needed time to think. He stood and returned to his loft. His head was spending after the long evening, first the plans about the shower, then Ms. Hills, and now Vivian.

Twenty-four hours passed, and he still hadn't heard from Vivian. When Jathrow entered his law building, Mr. Gee was there again. He was becoming a fixture. Jathrow rolled his eyes and wanted to ask questions; instead, he winked. Mr. Gee said, "That Jacey. She insisted on moving into her own house today." He chuckled; then he continued, "I dropped by their house, and poor Richard Jr. had men working all over the place. Even Ty was barking out orders, for he was trying to keep the rooms all clean and sanitary. The house looks great, and their land goes on and on. The brood will have plenty of acres on which to play."

"Do you think Jacey will return to films?" Jathrow asked.

"I doubt it. Even in her condition, she is so happy and content."

Ms. Hills stepped into the room and motioned Jathrow to his office. Of course, Mr. Gee was close on his heels. Jathrow opened the folding doors and was surprised to see the band equipment sit where his cherry desk once sat. The area flowed, joining the enormous east and west conference rooms. The streamers were hung. The flower arrangements were placed on the mini round tables and the high-back chairs were covered, all waiting for the guests. A cake table featured two sheet cakes trimmed with pink and blue booties. Ms. Hills pointed out the gift table, which overflowed with gifts. David entered with tray after tray of delicately cut sandwiches adding to the finger food. He stopped by them and said, "Jathrow, now your building serves more than one purpose." David continued on to the food tables.

When David entered again, Jathrow asked, "Are you really serving chicken wings?"

"I am. It's Jacey's request."

"What about Richard Jr. and his taste?" Jathrow poked David.

Laughing, David answered, "He can eat the finger foods or the grilled chicken that I'm serving. But tonight's event is all about Jacey and their babies. The old saying goes, 'A happy wife is a happy life!'"

Ty breathlessly tied on an apron and placed cloth napkins around the tables. He sprayed freshener and whizzed about the rooms. Stopping beside Jathrow, taking a breath, he said, "Jacey seems more like your daughter. You've always been there for her."

Jathrow swallowed. "She's a wonderful person.

15

Ty's eyes narrowed. "How about her mother. Have you two settled your differences? It's a fact that you are crazy for each other."

Ms. Hills once again returned, joining the men. She elbowed Jathrow. They walked outside where she introduced Jathrow to the parking lot attendants. Then she indicated, "Maybe one of your vehicles should be moved so you're not penned in." They walked further from listening ears. Ms. Hills placed a hand on his arm. "What gives between you and your friend, Vivian? I know Samuel has mentioned marriage to Vivian, but he's not pursuing marriage with her. And I've asked for your help. Well?"

Jathrow breathed, "I wasn't for sure Mr. Gee had asked for Vivian's hand in marriage. But I knew he gave her a ring a while back." Squinting his eyes, he said, "Nothing seems to indicate they are a twosome though." He laughed nervously. "How do you want me to help, Ms. Hills?"

Ms. Hills twisted her hands and looked around before speaking. "In case you haven't gotten the message, I like Mr. Gee, a lot. However, his hands are tied. I know he's interested in me, for things have heated up and are getting a little spicy. Since he is bound"—she rolled her large brown eyes when she said this—"you need to step up and use your manly charms on Vivian." She sighed. "Mr. Gee is not the man for her."

Jathrow threw his hands in the air. "As if life was that easy. You met Vivian. She is not a free-spirited type of woman. It's marriage—all in or nothing. Her and her high values." Frowning, he said, "I can ask her out, but speaking frankly, when we're together, it's hard to have a conversation without me looking stupid. My tongue gets stuck to the roof of my mouth."

"Have you asked Vivian what she wants from you, or are you assuming what you think she wants? Come on, Jathrow, time is of the essence here, and it will be entirely your fault if you and I are not happy in the end. Is pride standing in your way?" Ms. Hills nodded. "We know each other well enough now for you to call me Sandra." She turned and went back inside.

Jathrow went to his flat and took a cold shower. He wasn't any closer with decisions about Vivian, except for one: there definitely wouldn't be any marriage now or ever between Vivian and Mr. Samuel Gee. Looking in the mirror, he admitted, *What do I do? Sandra should be happy, and so should I. Now what am I going to do about the situation?*

Jathrow in a dapper black suit reentered the law building. Photographers were busy taking pictures of Jacey. She posed, sitting on a wide wing chair. To him, she looked absolutely miserable. Her face was round as a balloon and blotchy. Her legs were swollen, and her feet were shockingly puffy. He thought, *How could she glow and carry a genuine smile?*

He glanced through the crowd and saw the mayor, state representative, directors, other celebrities, and models. Anybody who was somebody attended. Jathrow saw the gift tables were loaded. He noticed Richard Jr. reach for Jacey's hand and lightly patted the barely recognizable surface. Jathrow wondered how much more could Jacey's skin possibly stretch.

He joined Jacey, kissed her forehead, and shook Richard Jr.'s hand. Photos snapped again. He moved to step aside when Jacey grabbed his hand. And she uttered, "Uncle Jathrow, get Mom. It's time to leave." Her eyes squinted, and her grip tightened. "Now!" Her face was distorted, lines showed on her forehead, eyes were squinting, and her lips were dry and stretched thin.

Jathrow nodded and rubbed his hand. He bobbed down the hallway, searching for Vivian. People stopped him. He caught Sandra's eye standing with Samuel. He motioned for her to come to him. He whispered, "I need to reach Vivian. Jacey wants to leave!" They made their way over to Vivian. Jathrow stopped and gazed in Vivian's soft green eyes.

"Your daughter appears to be in a lot of pain and wants you. She said something about leaving," Jathrow said.

Vivian reached for Jathrow's hand and darted inside.

He pushed, shoved, and bobbed through the crowd until they were by Jacey's side.

"What is it, precious?"

A tear slide down Jacey's face when she spoke, "My backaches and sharp pains are reaching my stomach. I sent my Richard to start the SUV. I need help leaving here."

Jathrow swished Jacey in his arms as though a feather. Soberly, he excused them from the people milling around. Vivian raised a hand and calmly stated, "Continue the party, folks."

The band conductor struck a cord and announced, "Let's dance."

Ms. Hills and Mr. Gee followed them outside.

Jathrow felt sticky as he carefully placed Jacey in the SUV. He glanced at Vivian questioningly as he helped her into the vehicle. She whispered in Jathrow's ear, "Jacey's water broke. We need to hurry to the hospital."

He pulled the door shut, seated himself on the other side next to Vivian. "Richard, get that silly grin off your face and drive. Don't stop at any red lights! Let's go, man, now!"

Jacey, not able to completely sit, motioned Jathrow over. He plastered a smile, feeling so out of place. He acted on her need and adjusted her seat so she was lying down. Vivian was saying soothing words. Jathrow glanced at Richard Jr. and saw sweat beads forming on his forehead. Jathrow bit his bottom lip. Things were serious. He flipped out his cell phone and called the hospital, making sure the doctor and nurses were on standby for Jacey.

Jacey held out her hand for Jathrow. He flinched as he patted her arm. "It's all right, Jacey. You're almost at the hospital." His blues eyes widened. "Don't push, Jacey! Jacey?" Jacey was unconscious.

Jathrow carefully wrenched his hand free from an unconscious Jacey. He pushed aside hair strands from her mouth. As the SUV stopped, he hopped from the vehicle and strode inside the ER's entrance demanding care for Jacey. He barked out orders and watched as the interns, doctor, and nurses moved in preparation for the incoming patient. Jathrow saw the orderlies open the back door of the SUV and removed seats. One said, "We should place her on a bed instead of carrying her in this condition."

Richard Jr. paled at the sight. He offered his arm to his wife, who stirred. She clung to him with wide eyes and asked, "Is it over?" And then she screamed as another pain shot through her.

"Don't push, Jacey. Wait. Breathe now. Your doctor is on his way." Jathrow grunted, "You're in good hands, and you'll be fine."

Jacey rolled her eyes and screamed, "Jathrow!"

He flinched at the sound; it was in higher pitches than he had ever heard from a human or animal! He strained to remain calm and answered, "I'm here, darling." He stroked her forehead, and the nurse in charged stopped at the bedside and gruffly asked, "What is your relationship, father or grandfather to be?"

He reddened while shaking his head and then reached for Richard Jr.'s shirttail. "He's the father to be. I'm only a close friend."

The white-haired female nurse pointed a finger to his chest and said, "Well then, you wait in the visitor's area!"

Jathrow walked backward as he watched the staff hurry Jacey off toward the delivery room. With hands in his pant's pockets, he went in the visitor's area, experiencing separation, a deep loneliness, and a lingering silence. He tried sitting and thumbing through magazines. He called David. The voice message picked up, and Jathrow left word, "David, update Ms. Hills and the guests about Jacey. She's in the delivery room now. And please oversee the party. I'll call or see you later." Jathrow slipped his cell phone in his pocket and picked up the same magazine.

A young lady in a stripped apron asked, "Would you like a cup of coffee?"

Jathrow smiled and nodded. "Yes. Thank you." *I've always had someone at my finger tips to talk with, but now, I'm the outsider.* Jathrow flung the magazine and walked to the nurses' station. "Is there any information on Jacey Pair?"

The young nurse smiled. "No."

Jathrow saw a Chapel sign and followed the path. He glanced inside the white room; only a few candles lit, and there was noticeable silence. He sank down on a wooden pew. The room emphasized his loneliness. Jathrow eyed a figurative cross. He hung his head, and tears fell. His heart was breaking, and he didn't understand until Vivian's face flashed before him. Jathrow would face his fears. He realized how mortal he was as a man. Jathrow knelt and prayed, " Creator of heaven and earth, the triplet's need safety, and Jacey needs protection and well-being." He sighed. "God, help me in facing Vivian." Jathrow promised he would attend church and give more if God would only work the situation out between Vivian and himself. Jathrow pulled his hair back and replaced the fastener. *I know I can't bargain or bribe You, but thanks for always being there and listening.*

A hand softly touched his shoulder "Are you all right, Jathrow?"

He swung his head, and his hair lightly touched her chin. "No. I'm far from being all right. I…oh, Vivian." He reached for her hands.

A nurse entered. "Are you Jathrow?"

He nodded and stood.

The nurse said, "Jacey is asking for you."

Jathrow received directions to the delivery room, and left Vivian sitting there.

The door opened, and Jathrow stepped in. "Hello, princess." He tenderly stroked her hair as he glanced over at a pale panicky Richard Jr. Jathrow saw the after-five shadow and bloodshot eyes. He touched Richard Jr.'s shoulder. "Man, take five. Go call your dad and mom, and there's a chapel down the hall." Jathrow returned his gaze on Jacey. "Now, my precious, how can I help you?"

Jacey slightly smiled and began huffing. Jathrow huffed with her. She reached for his hand and squeezed for dear life. He glanced at the monitor and watched the line graft up and then slowly down. Jacey's breathing eased. She said, "Will you be a godfather to my children?"

Jathrow let out a low whistle and stared at the frail person asking such a big thing. "Are you sure, Jacey?" He watched as another puffing was necessary.

She squeezed his hand as she huffed. " Get the doctor!"

Richard Jr. arrived as the doctor walked in. "Sir, you'll need to leave unless Jacey wants you to stay," the doctor said.

Jathrow bent and kissed her cheek. "I'll see you in a little while. Do as the doctor says." He waved a hand and stepped gladly outside the room. He assumed it wouldn't be long now. Jathrow joined Vivian in the waiting room. He suggested, "Perhaps you should be with Jacey?"

Vivian hunched her shoulder. "No. Jacey only wants her husband there. Besides we will be informed when the babies are born, and then I'll go in to check on her and the babies."

Richard Sr. walked in the hospital with Chloe on his arm. He bellowed, "Heard anything?"

Jathrow chuckled. He said, "Old man, I see where little Richard Jr. gets his patience from. The apple didn't fall far from the tree."

Chloe piped, "It sure didn't, Jathrow. I've always known."

Vivian placed an arm around Chloe and gave her a pat.

Moments passed into minutes and then reached into hours. Richard Sr. and Jathrow paced. Vivian and Chloe were like statues. A nurse entered the area, and silence fell upon the group, but she kept walking. The men resumed pacing, and the ladies leaned their heads back and closed their eyes. Heavy steps were in the hallway, and everyone placed their eyes on the man dressed in blues. He stopped short of the women. "Is there a Mrs. Rose, Mrs. Vivian Rose?"

Vivian jumped and cleared her throat. "I'm Vivian Rose." Chloe stood, and the two men soon huddled behind them. She blew a breath. "Is my daughter, Jacey Pair, all right? And the babies?"

The man removed his mask and introduced himself as Dr. Lilly. A slight smile appeared. "Mrs. Rose, your daughter is extremely tired, but fine. However she delivered quadruplets. The ultrasound only revealed one fast heart beat, and the babies were all piggyback. She and her husband have three healthy, fragile baby girls and one big baby boy. Congratulations! You may go back now and see Jacey. However, don't stay too long. The babies will all be in incubators."

Without word, all four rushed to see Jacey, Richard Jr., and the new arrivals. In whispers, they discussed the babies while Vivian touched her daughter's forehead with a kiss. The nurses moved out the four precious babies placed in incubators, all in a row. They were so small, yet beautiful. She followed. Vivian washed up and wore protective clothing, hoping she would be allowed to touch each of the babies' little hands.

The white-haired female nurse sternly whispered, "Visiting time is up. You can visit the babies in the special nursery wing."

Jathrow was about to leave. He asked Richard Jr., "Is there anything else needed for Jacey or the babies?"

Richard Jr. shook his head and uttered, "I really don't know, but pray."

Outside the room, the white-haired nurse gathered the four adults and said, "Jacey needs lots of rest. The four babies are doing well for being so small and premature. Now as exciting as this time is, please be considerate of each other and take turns in visiting Jacey over the next couple of days." The nurse locked eyes with Vivian. "Just while Jacey is gaining her strength." The veteran nurse left them, walking in the direction of the nurse's station.

Richard Sr. draped his arm around Chloe and said, "Let's all move ourselves to the cafeteria, where we will make plans."

126

Jathrow whispered to Vivian, "I'm leaving. I need to reach Mr. Gee and Ms. Hills. They will need a heads-up for the news release on Jacey and the babies." He frowned. "Hopefully they will ward off anxious, unwanted photographers."

Vivian nodded and leaned in. "Great idea. Go. See you soon." She touched his cheek. "Call me later." Still smiling, Vivian turned and joined their friends. They walked down the hallway.

Jathrow called a cab and, while waiting, tried Mr. Gee's cell phone and then Ms. Hills—both were busy. He asked the cabbie to drive fast. When he arrived at his office he was glad to see David and Ty still cleaning up. As he stepped into the hallway, he spotted Mr. Gee and Ms. Hills standing very close to each other, and they were in deep conversation. He cleared his throat, and both heads turned toward him. He said, "I tried to reach you both on your cells. Jacey delivered three girls and a boy. They all are fine. However, the press will need information. Heed them a warning. Perhaps you can stop the photographers. Suppose you work together on this project?"

Ms. Hills brown eyes brighten as she looped arms with Mr. Gee, who spoke, "We're on it."

16

Jathrow walked into the makeshift kitchen and motioned to David. "Walk with me outside?"

David nodded. "Meet you out front in a minute or two."

Jathrow hoisted up the collar of his Italian-made suit. David joined Jathrow, and he asked, "How do you know when the right woman has come along?"

David bunched his brows and said, "Friend, how are you sleeping?"

Jathrow moaned, "You know the word *forever* scares me to death. All I think about is Vivian." The wind stirred Jathrow's hair. He opened his mouth, paused, and glanced in David direction. "I know this sounds lame. But I've never met a woman I've wanted more than Vivian. David, I've distanced myself from her out of respect. She's my friend."

David shook his head and placed a hand on Jathrow's back. "Have you talked with God about your feelings toward Vivian? Have you been honest about your feelings with Vivian, stating your true feelings for her?"

Jathrow hung his head.

"Friend, talk with Vivian. After all, you two aren't sixteen anymore. And I know for a fact she cares for you. What is wrong with staying with a woman like Vivian forever?"

❧❦❧

Dawn was cracking. Jathrow and God wrestled through the night, and Jathrow's spirit was broken. On bended knees, he asked Jesus for forgiveness and to reunite their walk.

He also asked for help and wisdom in his work and to give him guidance when it came to Vivian. He noticed his cell phone was blinking green. He listened to the messages from Ms. Hills. He knew to send Vivian flowers. He was also to send a planter to Jacey. He chuckled when Ms. Hills said this message: "I know you're on the right track, boss. I'll see you at the hospital, and I'm with Samuel!"

Jathrow walked to his flat and peered around. He was pleased with the modern design, but thoughts haunted him about Vivian's homey cottage. He gathered a change of clothes and took a steamy hot shower. Forty-five minutes later, he was dressed. Jathrow picked up the phone, "Hello, is this the florist? This is Jathrow Mowey. I would like to order a planter to be sent to Jacey Pair at Drum's Hospital." He tapped the counter and felt sweat beads on his forehead. "Please deliver two dozen purple roses to Vivian Rose at her cottage." He hung up the receiver, stretched his arms, and breathed deep. He noticed he was smiling and at peace.

Several days passed. As he lay sprawled in bed, he heard the community church bell strike nine. He needed to call the hospital and check on Jacey and the babies. Next he called Vivian as he headed out the door. "Hello, Vivian."

"Jathrow?"

The wind soared in the car window and muffled his voice. He asked, "Vivian, after church would you join me for lunch?"

Vivian screeched, "Are you coming to church?"

Jathrow looked at his cell, for he was disconnected from Vivian. His bars were completely used up. He tossed the phone in the glove compartment and said, "I'll ask Vivian at church if she was free to have lunch." He huffed as he pulled into the church's lot. He had to circle the row and wait for someone to pull out so he could park. Jathrow opened his trunk and found a Bible and blew dust from it. He thought, *My new beginning.* He viewed his male friends with their wives sitting four rows from the front with Vivian. He squared his shoulders, plastered on a smile, and greeted the people as he walked forward.

Vivian lifted the edge of her hat and frowned. She nudged David to move down a seat. Jathrow stepped in and stood beside her. He opened a songbook to the announced page and offered to share it with Vivian.

David and Ty's eyes shifted to Jathrow, and their mouths gaped. The music began, and Jathrow's tenor voice didn't miss a note. All were seated. Jathrow opened his Bible to the Psalms and listened attentively. He nodded his head and said a few amens.

When the service was over, he stepped from the pew and offered his arm to Vivian. She touched his arm and matched his stride. Outside, Jathrow asked, "Vivian, will you have lunch with me?" "Follow me home. I'll accept your offer for lunch."

He noticed his friends' puckered brows. *I can't blame our friends for being skeptical at my newfound sincerity in church or in Vivian.* Jathrow tipped his hat and slid under the wheel of the red BMW. He was only too glad to follow his lifelong friend. He waited in the car at her request. Soon they were on their way into the city. It was a long drive. They talked about the new babies. Both laughed at the surprised parents and how the unexpected life of four had changed everything. Vivian said, "Richard Jr. has been a real trooper. He has hired a full-time nanny and acts as if all is under control."

Jathrow said, "He's in for the time of his life. I am happy they at least had one boy. He's going to need someone in his corner." Jathrow shook his head and continued, "Wow, all those girls." Jathrow parked and escorted Vivian inside to the Main Hotel Restaurant.

Jathrow motioned for the waitress and said, "Vivian, coffee, hot tea, or would you care for iced tea?"

"Iced tea. Also honey, please."

Jathrow nodded. "Coffee for me, black."

In the background, jazz music was playing softly. The restaurant's square tables were covered in white linens, which held tall centerpieces. He thought, *Seasonal.*

Vivian touched his arm. "I want to thank you for the lovely roses, but purple?"

"What other color would I send you?"

She blushed as she stumbled to speak, "Well, Jathrow, certain colors do have certain meaning."

He winked. The waitress placed their salads down and asked about grinding pepper. Neither he nor Vivian answered, for they weren't paying attention to the waitress. Their eyes had locked on each other. Silence had fallen, and heat was rising. He watched as her eyes changed from their known softness to a fiery liquefied pool. Jathrow forced his eyes to focus elsewhere. He needed to slow his tempo and be proper with

Vivian. He reached for a slice of bread and then blotted his mouth. He took a sip of coffee, trying to slide down a bite of salad. He glanced her way and waited for her to speak. He saw that she had stiffened and she was distancing herself once again from him like she had done so many times before.

Jathrow panicked; he wasn't letting her slip away. No, not this time. He stood, kissed Vivian full on the mouth, and then knelt on one knee. Sweating, he heard a strange voice—his—saying, "Vivian, you're special." His searching blue eyes cast upward as he rushed the words, "There has never been anyone else who has ever meant more to me than you do." He reached for her hand. "I want there to be an…us in a rightful way." He blew out air. "Vivian. Am I making any sense to you?"

Vivian green eyes widened. She waited, but he didn't say those three wonderful words, I love you. She shook off his hand and stood. "Get up, Jathrow! People are staring, and they'll think you're being serious, proposing."

He didn't move, his blue eyes narrowed, and his hands were clammy. Jathrow reached for her hand again, pleading, "I am asking for your hand in marriage. I'm sorry I don't have a proper ring to offer, but here is my law graduate ring. I hadn't plan on asking you today—well, not right here right now—but come on, Vivian, take pity on me down here. This is my very first time in proposing. Please accept me. Marry your old friend!"

Vivian pulled her hand free again, and tears stained her cheeks.

His heart got stabbed. He noticed a redness begin from her neck and somehow darkened on her face. He had embarrassed her in public. Jathrow stood, tossed her his car keys, and muttered, with hands curled into fists at his sides, "Sorry, Vivian. I thought this is what you wanted from me." He reached into his pocket and flipped bills on the table. He saw people gawking, and some were even pointing at them. A photo was snap as Jathrow stalked from the restaurant. He retrieved the camera, pulled the film, and splattered the shell. He yelled at the paparazzi, "Can't you stay out of my life?"

Jathrow couldn't keep from looking back where he saw Vivian's frail hand lift in the air. Jathrow stomach juices were in his throat. He needed to regroup from the raw rejection. He ran and didn't stop until he reached the town's crossroads. His whole body shook. He loosened his silk tie and wadded it in his side pocket and let the long-held tears fall.

Had he been at the town's crossroads only moments, minutes, or maybe hours, he didn't know. Jathrow flipped open his cell phone and called Ms. Hills. He had one bar left.

"Hello?"

"Ms. Hills. Call the airport immediately and make arrangements for me to fly to LA today. And send a car for me at the town's crossroads. Ms. Hills?"

"Yes, Mr. Mowey."

He blew out a long breath . "Don't tell anyone about this call. Or, or I'll fire you!" His voice quivered as he commanded. "I'm waiting!"

He saw a car slowing, and the driver was Mr. Gee. He stepped out, opened the car door, and a humble Jathrow slid in.

Mr. Gee said, "I was with Ms. Hills when you called." Mr. Gee adjusted the side mirror and asked, "Airport?"

"Yes."

He reached for the car phone and pushed in Stan's number. Jathrow heard a burly voice asked, "Jathrow, is that you?"

Jathrow sighed and cleared his throat. "It is. I read the file you sent me about the possible merger between the Wares and Borons . You know I handled both their divorces, and they were not civil. What were you thinking wanting to combine their businesses?"

He heard Stan's chair screeched. Stan moaned, "It's Sunday. The Wares have a new product, but the Borons have the clients. If neither budge, the money flow stops. They haven't listened to reason about anything until I presented this business deal to them, assuring them both parties would be equals. Some matters are a mess no matter what one does."

"I'm on my way to LA, so set up a meeting with both parties. And be sure to have each family represented with a lawyer. I have an idea. Stan, is the efficiency apartment still available?"

"Yes, the apartment is available. What do you mean you have an idea?"

Jathrow laughed. "Don't let anyone know I'm coming, and if for any reason someone from Virginia calls, you haven't heard from me! Bye, Stan."

Jathrow saluted Samuel as he checked in at the airport. The steward informed him he had forty-five minutes to wait before liftoff. Jathrow thanked her and rushed inside the airport's men's clothing store. He gathered a suitcase and two business suits, one navy blue and the other solid black. He had the sales clerk select two shirts, silk ties, and socks. He added briefs and T-shirts. Jathrow scanned the rack like a madman and found a casual jacket. He added two polo shirts and a pair of Levi skinny jeans. At the counter, he handed the person behind the cash register his trusty plastic and signed his name. Jathrow slammed his new purchases into the suitcase and carried it onto the plane. Jathrow stretched out his long legs and tilted the seat backward.

His mind wondered as his heart ached. He visualized the pain in Vivian's wide green eyes, the look. His insides were twisting. *So much for easing into a conversation about my undying love. I acted unforgivable.* He would apologize to Vivian someday. But for now, he would as always bury himself in the only life he knew. Jathrow jerked when someone tapped on his shoulder. He saw the drink sitting on his tray. He breathed deep, tipped his head, and swallowed the bitter liquid.

Vivian trembled as she drove Jathrow's BMW to the cottage. Her chest ached with sorrow. Vivian wanted to drive the hidden feelings of Jathrow and her loneliness away. But tears emerged as if a volcano had erupted. She let out a heavy sigh and finally parked Jathrow's car in front of the cottage. Inside, the quietness was unbearable.

The night was dark, and the stars and moon were hidden. The winds howled as the waves crashed, but Vivian was determined to stay on the beach. She positioned her knees under her chin, folded her arms, and let the tears continue. Vivian shook her head, for she could not erase the picture of Jathrow's face—those sad blue eyes. She looked out to the waters. *His sweet gentle kiss still lingers on my lips.* She wiped the tears. *I wasn't expecting Jathrow to kneel on one knee and propose. Why had I freaked out? Was it because my obligation to Samuel Gee isn't completely broken? Or did I still not trust or believe in Jathrow enough that he wanted a true commitment?* She cried harder. *Oh why, couldn't he have said those three little words, I love you?* She blew out a breath. *I never saw his blue eyes narrow so quickly, and for a split second, there appeared an iron coldness in his eyes. They turned even a deeper color of blue, almost slate.* She shivered at the image. *I was amazed at the warmth and vulnerability Jathrow showed me earlier, and my, how quickly it all vanished.*

Vivian adjusted her hands and sat in dismay, rocking back and forth to the rhythm of water, knowing she alone was responsible for Jathrow's fun-loving manner to immediately slump from her rejection, and he fled. She bit her lip. *How will I ever explain or give my answer about marriage to him. He may never know, my answer could have been a yes. Darn purple roses. I should just throw them out!*

The tide touched her feet, and the water was cold. Vivian unfolded from the sand and carried her slippers across the sandy road into the house. She brewed some chamomile tea and sat at her desk in the dark. The hour was late, and she hesitated in calling Jathrow, for she couldn't face rejection. She prayed and sought guidance. *Help me!* Feeling somewhat at peace she decided to write him a note and send it by courier. She penned,

> My dearest Jathrow, we have come full cycle in life, me wanting you and you wanting me. Although, all these years, I dreamed secretly of a marriage with you, I never imagined you were that interested in pursuing a marriage with me. I did have high hopes though and trust that we wouldn't be as ships passing in the night; however, you have always somehow seemed to set sail without me. I'm just so poor at explaining my meaning. You would think as a writer my words would not be hindered.
>
> Let me try again. I am sorry you misread and misunderstood my reaction at the hotel restaurant for not wanting to make a commitment to you. I have a few loose ends to take care of, but I truly do want to accept your marriage proposal, if the offer still stands. But what I don't want is for you to feel obligated in asking me again because of our friends or their persistence of there being an us. Your proposal must come from within your heart.
>
> I know we have a true passion for one another, so I pray and anticipate we will be able to work through this awkward situation. We need to talk. Call, write, text, e-mail—I don't care, just please answer me.
>
> Love always and again thanks for the purple roses, your Vivian.

She folded the letter and enclosed it to the envelope. She addressed it to his flat. Vivian swiftly called the courier company and breathed a sigh of relief, knowing her words were on their way to her beloved,

Jathrow. She sat in the oversized chair near the phone and waited. Her eyes became heavy, and sleep invaded.

Nights turned into days and then into weeks, and slowly three months had past and still no word from Jathrow. Vivian kept busy, devoting her time to the babies and her writings. She refused to talk or inquire information about Jathrow from Jacey or friends. Vivian was also waiting for her latest novel to arrive. Mr. Gee, whom she had distanced herself from, arranged another book release party.

David had been notified, and the invitations and press release had been taken care of. Within a week, all but one RSVP had been accounted for.

The book signing was a casual affair with plenty of finger foods and a live band. David, along with Ty and Richard Sr., decorated the gardens. Mr. Gee arranged for flowers to be flown in from a warm climate. Ty, Mr. Gee, and David placed a display table in the hallway for Vivian's new books.

Vivian wore her purchased brightly colored flowered patio dress and matching hat. She saw guests had arrived, and she flitted from room to room, speaking with each person. After an hour, the bandleader made the announcement, "Ladies and gentlemen, please gather to the display table. Ms. Vivian Rose will sign your selections for a short while." Vivian signed for an hour. Mr. Gee signaled for the band to play again. The floor was crowded, and the dancers bumped into one another. More people popped in and wanted Vivian's book. The band broke for another singing. An hour later, her daughter made an appearance. The bandleader announced, "Intermission."

17

The crowd shifted and swooped in on Jacey. Over the next thirty minutes, she answered questions about the babies. She whispered in Mr. Gee's ,ear and he went to the front door and helped Richard Jr. in with the four darlings. It was the babies' first public appearance, and many pictures were snapped. Vivian beamed and watched behind Jacey as the band played their last few songs before the party ended.

All the socialites were gone. Vivian gathered two books and with checks in hand and waited while the crew wrapped up.

Mr. Gee walked over to Vivian. "Do you need me any longer?"

"No, Samuel, but thank you for another successful book launch." She touched his arm. "Samuel, my dear Samuel, you're a wonderful man, but you must know by now my feelings for you remain only professional. There really isn't any easy way for me to say..." She slipped the box holding the ring . She looked into his warm, kind eyes. "I thought this over for the pass five months. And thank you for never pressuring me after you left the ring on my desk. Samuel, you're free." Leaning in, she said, "Be off with you. I now see Ms. Hills is still here, perhaps, waiting?"

Mr. Gee cleared his throat and blushed.

Vivian whispered, "It's all right, Samuel."

He patted Vivian's arm, smiled, and kissed her cheek. Vivian noticed Samuel appeared taller, straighter as he waved and walked beamingly toward Ms. Hills.

Jacey touched her mother's face. "Mother, your book signing was more successful than the last one." She glanced around the room to see who might be listening. No one was. "I'm sorry things didn't work out with you and Mr. Samuel Gee."

Vivian patted her daughter's hand.

"I need to take care of the babies. Call me tomorrow, Mom, and we will plan a lunch date."

Vivian hugged her daughter and thanked her for coming. She closed the front door and shivered. Vivian wrapped her arms around herself and walked toward the kitchen. She held her breath as she heard rustling. *Maybe Jathrow's here.*

But it was Ty. He held out her coat and said, "I didn't mean to frighten you. Here slip this on and step outside."

"Why?"

He didn't answer. Ty held opened the backdoor and gave Vivian a gentle nudge. She stepped down to the patio and placed her folded hands to her heart. There stood Jathrow. He was dressed in black slacks, a knee-length camel tweed coat, matching scarf, and a hat. He opened his arms, and she ran to him. She peered upward and saw his beard was more than a shadow. It pricked her face. Jathrow held her at arm's length and in a whisper, cried, "I arrived here in Virginia an hour ago and went to the flat where I received your letter." He blew out a breath. "My Vivian, I need you to understand why I left for California." He squeezed her shoulders. "After I had embarrassed you in a very public place, asking for your hand in marriage, I believed my feelings for you were one-sided."

"What feelings?"

He kissed her long and hard.

"Jathrow, I've always loved you. Don't you dare ever run from me again!"

Jathrow moved his hands into her hair, bent down, and whispered, "Who's running?"

Vivian was sure he could feel her heart pound. She wanted a clear understanding of what Jathrow expected from her. She reached for his hands. "Where do you see us in this relationship?"

Jathrow anchored her yet closer, kissing her slow, then deepening the kiss. His passion left no doubt as he raised his head and breathed happily, "Get me to the church!"

Vivian touched her swollen lips. "You sure?"

Stepping back, he looked into her gentle, trustworthy green eyes and said, "Just you try and get rid of me!"

The corners of Vivian's mouth raised, and more tears flowed.

She held out her left hand, emphasizing her ring finger and squealed, "Where's the ring?"

Jathrow smiled, avoiding the question, and with tilted head, he said, "Can we go inside?"

Hand in hand, they walked into the kitchen. There sat two steaming mugs of black coffee and a piece of pumpkin pie, laced with homemade whipped cream. Not a word was spoken. Then the forks clunked. Jathrow lifted from his seat and carried the plates, forks, and cups to the sink. Looking out the window, he asked, "Vivian, where do you want to live? Here in Virginia or in California?"

She placed a hand on his back, then tugged his blond ponytail. "Wherever is fine with me."

He lifted Vivian and swung her around. His bright blue eyes turned smoky hot as he nuzzled and said, "Don't make me wait long." He ran his long finger beside her cheek. "Do you want me to call the minister?"

She shakily handed Jathrow the phone and rattled off the number. She was still waving her finger. Jathrow tossed his head back and laughed. "His Reverence Paul, please? Yes, I know the hour, but this is important, life or death." He held his ground until all necessary counseling arrangements were made for him and Vivian.

Hanging the receiver up, he noticed the fire was kindling in the other room. Jathrow took Vivian's hand to his lips and walked with her into the living room. He reached into his coat pocket and slid to one knee. He said, "Vivian, this ring belonged to my grandmother who passed it down to my mother when she married." Jathrow sucked in air, his chest began tightening, but he pushed through. "Would you, Vivian, do me the honor of making me the happiest man on the earth and accept this ring?" He breathed out and added, "Become my wife. I love you."

Trembling, she nodded as she let the tears flow. Jathrow remained on one knee, still not placing the ring on her finger. His brows narrowed as he said, "I'm waiting. Is the nod a yes?"

Vivian knelt and hugged him. She whispered, "Jathrow, you love me. I loved you, and yes, I still love you." Her reddened eyes brightened. "Yes yes yes." Vivian wiggled her ring finger again. "I never knew you were given your grandmother's ring. It's beautiful. I admire it so."

Jathrow relaxed. "The blue diamond is a carat in size, and it is surrounded by Rose Hill gold laurel leaves."

"Ah, so breathtaking."

He glided the ring on the ring finger of the left hand. He aired, "Wow, it's a snug fit. I don't ever want you to take it off even when we wed."

Vivian gasped. "Oh, Jathrow, you are an old romantic at heart."

They hugged and kissed some more. The front door bell dinged. Jathrow rose, offering Vivian a hand. He shook his head. "Who do you think could be here at this hour?" Together they opened the door.

"Surprise!" The whole gang was there.

David passed by Jathrow and Vivian, entering the cottage. He said, "Ms. Hills called before the book signing, stating Jathrow was back. But during the evening, when you didn't show, I began to wonder. I did think it strange when Ty waved me on to leave, because he didn't have a ride. I decided to wait down the road, and sure enough, Ty came walking."

Ty shrugged his shoulders. The doorbell dinged again. Jathrow opened the door. Mr. Gee stepped in, holding Ms. Hills's hand. Ms. Hills announced, "You're not the only man showing chivalry." Ms. Hills pulled Mr. Gee closer and lifted her left hand. "See."

Everyone cheered. Richard Sr. asked, "Say, Mr. Gee, where will you both be residing?"

Jathrow interrupted, "My flat will soon be available."

Vivian, wide-eyed, grasped Jathrow's hand. She tugged on his sleeve. "So are we living at the cottage?"

He bent, kissing her publicly, and said, "There's no place I'd rather be. I'm home."

With the announcements, Ty, Richard Sr., and David tossed their hats in the air. Then the clapping and cheering began. David said, "Well, Jathrow, when's the long-overdue wedding date?"

"We made plans with Reverend Paul earlier tonight. We begin our premarital counseling tomorrow—well, later today." He raised Vivian's hand for their friends to see the ring. "We can be married within six weeks!" Jathrow's eyes didn't move from Vivian.

David asked, "Mr. Gee, do you have any ideas?"

Ms. Hills hooted, "Yes, we do. I've arranged for a flight to Las Vegas later today."

139

Jathrow patted Mr. Gee on the back. He gave Ms. Hills a kiss on the cheek. Smiling, he said, "Mr. Samuel Gee, welcome to our family of friends."

Mr. Gee said, "Just call me Samuel from now on." He glanced Jathrow's way. "Do you have another place to live? Sandra and I will be back in three or four days. I have my checkbook out."

Everyone shouted. The doorbell dinged again. Jathrow moved to the door. He half cried, "Jacey Litten Pair, what are you and Richard Jr. doing here?" He frowned and instantly asked, "Are the babies all right?"

Richard Jr. nodded. "Jathrow, all the babies are fine, but news has traveled. We had to see for ourselves. Is it true?"

Vivian embraced her daughter. "Thanks for coming by, but how did you hear?"

Jacey pointed at Jathrow. "He stopped by our place and asked for my blessing in asking you to marry him."

Vivian's hands flew to the air. "Jathrow, you thought of everything."

David clapped Jathrow on the back. "It's about time, my friend."

Jathrow reached into his pocket and took a key off his key ring and tossed it to Samuel. He, said, "Pay me when you two get back." He glanced at the couple and asked, "You need any witnesses?"

Vivian stomped her foot. "Don't you get any ideas, mister. We're getting married in the church. I've waited far too long for you."

David answered firmly, "Hear, hear." He then turned to Samuel, adding, "Man, you are on your own."

Sandra rolled her eyes and said, "Men, I'll take real good care of him." She winked and pushed Samuel toward the door, pausing long enough to say, "Congratulations, Jathrow, Vivian. See you in a week."

An hour later, friends and family left. Jathrow sat on a chair, pulling Vivian with him. He calmly asked, "Can I bunk out here?"

Vivian gave him a lingering kiss and pressed up, answering, "You, sir, need to call a cab."

Jathrow stood with hands on hips, staring in disbelief. She continued, "It's been thirty-two years of on and off with you. So what's another six weeks of waiting for me. It won't hurt you!" She handed him the phone . They both laughed.

But Jathrow stopped in the doorway and reached for his bride-to-be.

He placed a hand under her chin and gave her a peck. He tipped his hat, and the corners of his mouth lifted into a wide smile. He entered the cab and told the cabbie his firm's address.

He decided sleep was not in the making. Jathrow punched in the code and walked down the hall to his office. He slipped off his tie, jacket, and shoes. He saw it was almost sunrise and chuckled. "I'll sure make good use of the Murphy Bed David insisted was a must-have for any office."

After a few hours had passed, Jathrow reached in the tote bag and pulled out his running gear .He shook out his old faithful jogging jacket and hit the road. Jathrow covered mile after mile. *Will passion and our friendship be enough?* He ran a little farther and stopped. *I needed to speak with Vivian of my concern on our lasting marriage.*

Jathrow felt the wind whipping around his face; he paced himself. He ran another mile and reasoned, *Is my fear coming from being a lawyer serving in the divorce department? Or am I jumpy like any other man getting married?"* Jathrow caught his breath, and rationalization entered, *I have three best friends who appear content and happy in their married life. I wonder if they ever had any anxiety of this forever-after stuff.* His stomach rolled. He was making himself miserable with all the what ifs. Jathrow let out a long sigh. *As a bachelor, I was always in control of my feelings and my choice to be or not to be with different women. But Vivian—she's different, special.* He realized she had woven herself into his soul. *Vivian is every woman wrapped into one person. And her attributes are many—she is good, kind, caring, loving, and honest.* He smiled. *Vivian is attractive, and that spunky red hair, oh those green large eyes.* Jathrow thought, *It scares the socks off me to be so empowered by the love of a woman.* He was drawn to Vivian like a moth is to a flame. Jathrow laughed and cried. Sweat beaded on his forehead. He understood, for the first time in his life, why he had never gotten close with any female. *No woman had ever compared to Vivian.*

He finally realized that trust issues came in his early years when raised by a teenage, widowed mother. She was kind, a loving soul, but was dirt poor and trusted every man she met. That's why I left Virginia as a young adult, driven in my soul to become successful. He pledged to provide for his mother, which could only be done through power, money, and him staying single. Jathrow realized now how he had depended on friends for love and support, especially when his mother's untimely death from pneumonia came. Jathrow carried guilt and pushed for more power and independence.

His mind was cleared after the morning jog. Jathrow returned to his office, sat down, and with paper and pen in hand, wrote,

My love, I want to share the hidden secrets of my heart. Fear began while we were in high school and again when I arrived at your first wedding. I watched you pledged yourself to the famous Dr. Rose. I reflected upon myself and reasoned, I had success and was gaining notability, but compared to your doctor, I was a nobody in society. I did arrive, early, on the day of your wedding to tell you my feelings for you. I wanted to plead with you not to marry the good doctor. However, when I witnessed the bliss on your face and walked through his decorated mansion, I knew I was out of my league. You were right in saying you saw me after your wedding vows. I was such a coward. Vivian, you were beautiful in the lace gown. I wept, in secret, from the corner store, away from eyes view. Then when news came about Jacey's birth, I was envious; she wasn't ours. I didn't think to bring God into the equation until much, much later in life.

Dear, I took Jacey under my wing professionally so I could learn more about you although I didn't understand my reasoning at the time. After the doctor died, I wanted a chance with you, but your life was here in Virginia and mine was in California, so I withdrew—again. And to be honest, I only wanted to sleep around with you. I dared not wished for more. You had become accomplished to the world as an author.

Vivian, God whipped me, and I reached a mental and spiritual low. When I heard of Mr. Gee's interest in you, I thought I would die. My love, I will never be worthy of you until the day I die. From the bottom of my heart, I want to thank you for saying yes to a marriage with me. I truly love you so!

Always yours,

L, Jathrow.

The letter was contained in his front jacket pocket as he drove to Vivian's place. He needed nothing left unsaid. He realized Vivian might need more time in reviewing her commitment to him. In two strides he reached the front door and knocked. There wasn't any answer. He ran to the gardens, looking around, and there she stood wearing the pink floppy hat. He placed his hand to his chest and smiled. She was beautiful. Vivian took his breath away.

Vivian turned and graced him with a smile.

"How wonderful to see you, darling." She removed her hat and came closer and saw Jathrow's eyes, she asked, "What going on?"

Jathrow kicked the ground and handed over his letter. "Vivian, you need to know the truth about me, my past thoughts on you…us, if there is to be a life of us together."

She stepped nearer, but he stepped back and lifted his hand. He tilted his head and said, "After you have time to dwell on the written words I've penned, call me." He pinched his nose and added, "I'll always love you." Jathrow grabbed her and kissed her long and hard. "I've already spoken with the reverend."

18

Vivian's jaw dropped as she read and reread Jathrow's letter. She crushed it to her chest, and let the tears fall. Her stomach twisted in knots for she felt her beloved's tortured pain from his past. She knew from her life experiences how position, power, money, and pride all played into society, especially in his. She eased into a chair. *If only Jathrow had asked me when I was younger, I would have chosen to stay dirt poor with him and loved every minute of it.*

The afternoon somehow passed. Vivian challenged herself and dressed with a mission in mind. She contacted the reverend and went to his office. A force stronger than life itself drove her like never before. Afterward, she met up with David and Ty and then set up an appointment with Richard Sr. She was amazed when reaching Ms. Hills and was please when they conferenced a call with Jacey. Arrangements were made, and she knew God would work everything out.

Jathrow had a room in town at the Richmond Hotel. He received an unexpected business call came from Stan. "Jathrow, take the next flight out. You're needed back in LA tomorrow morning for a meeting."

Jathrow walked down to his office and found a note on his desk. It was from his former secretary, now married Ms. Samuel Gee.

> Jathrow, Samuel and I are traveling. Should you need me, I'm only
> a phone call away.

He tapped his phone and said, "I'll make my own flight arrangements." He forwarded an e-mail to the new receptionist, Lynn Carly and also left an office voice message of his agenda.

Christmas was in two days. Vivian was unable to reach Jathrow, so she called Stan Trout. After a brief exchange, she said, "Mr. Trout, I need you to have Jathrow at the Richmond Baptist Church in Virginia by Christmas Eve no later than 7:15 p.m."

"And why do I need to have Jathrow in Virginia?"

She sighed. "We're getting married, but he doesn't know it yet."

Laughing, Stan said, "I'll get right on that matter. Thanks for calling."

Vivian wanted to say more, only Stan had dismissed her. Before the receiver at the other end was placed on the phone's cradle, she overheard him saying, "Thanks for stopping by the office, Jathrow. We have an urgent business matter to discuss."

❧❀☙

Jathrow shook his head as the plane landed in Virginia with him and Stan. He didn't understand Stan's sudden interest in the state, especially at five o'clock on Christmas Eve, but who was he to question? The men shared a light meal, and Stan mentioned he needed some alone time. Jathrow squirmed when he listened to his phone message, from Vivian "Jathrow, call me."

He run a finger around his neck and pushed in Vivian's number. "Hello, Jathrow, are you in town?"

"I am."

"We need to talk. I'll be back in touch." The line went silent.

He inhaled a long breath and took a shower. He thought, *When did she want to talk and where are we to meet?* It was now six o'clock in the evening. Jathrow dressed in his new imported black suit and rapped on Stan's hotel door. He knocked again, but there wasn't any answer. Shrugging, he walked to the front desk to leave Stan a message. However, Jathrow was handed a note from Stan Trout.

> I borrowed your car. Meet me at the church at 7:00 p.m. I'm looking forward to hear a quaint service. It's been a long, long time. Hurry.
>
> Signed Stan Trout

Jathrow went back to his room and grabbed a topcoat. He broke into a smile. "Look at this town. What a sight." The wind blew and the decorated lights, Christmas wreaths, and trees were swaying back and forth. He flung his coat collar up and walked briskly. When he entered the church grounds, Reverend Paul pulled Jathrow aside. "Are you ready?"

Jathrow's brows bunched. He then was clapped on his back as the Reverend continued, "Accepting a status in married life is a serious business. Congratulations, Jathrow."

Jathrow paled. "Who's getting married? What's going on?"

Reverend Paul took Jathrow's coat and stated, "Marriage, my man." The reverend's smile broadened.David entered the side room with Stan trailing behind. They were talking among themselves. David glanced at Jathrow and chuckled. "Friend, Vivian made sure you didn't run this time."

Stan thrust Jathrow a zippered bag and said, "Here, change."

David helped unzip the bag. "Get into this black tux. Ty, Richard Sr., and Richard Jr. will be joining us."

Jathrow slipped in one leg shakily and then the other. "I'm doing this, why?"

David snapped his suspenders. "For love. I'm walking the bride down the aisle."

Jathrow grew paler and squeaked, "I'm really getting married. To Vivian?"

Stan patted him on the cheek. "It's about time, don't you think?"

David added, "Vivian has waited on you for over thirty years."

Jathrow tilted his head. Music was playing. Sweat beads formed on his forehead.

Ty asked, "Do you know when all this was planned?"

Jathrow in a low choking whisper, "I thought Vivian and I were to meet with the reverend first."

Richard Sr. helped straighten Jathrow's bow tie, laughing. Richard Jr. handed him his polished black shoes. Stan stated, "Vivian showed your letter to Jacey declaring your love, and you know women when they put their heads together." Stan snorted. "Within just two hours everything was planned."

Jathrow shuffled to his feet and looked around. "Men, didn't any of you think or care enough to inform me of my special day?"

Richard Sr. brushed Jathrow's jacket and said, "You're at your very best when you're presented with a challenge."

Reverend Paul motioned to Jathrow, then said, "You did ask me to marry you and Vivian. It's time, son. Follow me."

Jathrow felt his Adam's apple go up then down. And then there were steps. As if in slow motion Stan stood to the right and Richard Sr. followed and then Ty. Richard Jr. joined his wife with their foursome; the girls were flower girls and the boy the ring bearer.

Jathrow let out a held breath and watched Reverend Paul step through the doorway and take his place. He then proceeded after him and halted when he saw the massive crowd sitting and standing around the church. Stan nudged him, and Richard Sr. took his arm and moved forward. Jathrow stood in place, facing the crowd. He was amazed, seeing business clients, friends, and socialites from around the world, sitting in the church pews. The other men adjusted their shoulders and took their position. Jathrow's blue eyes widened when he saw Mrs. Sandra and Samuel Gee sitting on the bride's side.

The photographers moved in different directions to make sure all angles were covered. Jathrow threw his hand to cover his eyes. *Snap, snap, snap*, went the bulbs. He blinked. The organ began, and his heartbeat faster. *I can do this. I want this.*

A shriveled-looking aged woman pounded the keys, producing a shrilling melody. He watched as if frozen while Richard Jr. and Jacey escorted their children down the aisle in a small white wagon draped with purple and pink streamers, which trailed behind. More pictures were snapped, and the crowd oohed.

The floor runner was covered by lavender and pink rose petals.

Jathrow shifted and focused his eyes watching Chloe walk down the aisle, following Doreen. Both women wore free-flowing vibrant pink dresses. Jacey, who was wearing a two-toned bright-pink dress with purple overlay, moved from Richard Jr.'s side and walked, taking her place next to Chloe.

Jathrow slid a finger around his shirt collar. Sweat beads formed on his forehead. He leaned over and whispered in Stan's ear, "The ring. I don't have a ring."

Richard Sr. thumbed his watch pocket while lifting on his heels and toes. He said, "I have the ring. Mrs. Sandra Gee charged the matching bands on your company card."

The organ stopped, and the room went silent. Six trumpet players walked to the front's center and sounded. On cue, a plump rounded woman came forward and clasped her gloved hands. In a brilliant perfect pitch, she sang "I Love You Truly." Women were dabbing their eyes, and the men moved in their seats uneasily. More pictures were snapped.

The organ made a grinding noise, and the aged woman pumped the pedals again. The notes hummed in tradition and were much overexaggerated. Reverend Paul raised his hands and motioned everyone to stand. Everyone turned and faced the bride. Vivian was breathtaking. She was beautiful beyond words in a pastel pink floor-length layered laced dress with full veil, which swished as she walked. Her green eyes sparkled as she walked with David. They continued to the front, and the pair was odd to watch. David, who was six feet six inches, nearly swallowed up Vivian's small five-feet-four-inch frame. Her lively red locks shaped her face, and her green eyes widened as she stood near Jathrow.

He breathed. *How could anyone her age, fifty-two, appear so youthful, firm, and delicious.* His stomach churned.

Reverend Paul motioned for everyone to be seated. He read Psalms 95 and spoke about Thanksgiving. He then motioned for Jathrow to speak his own commitment vows.

"I, Jathrow Mowey, have always loved you, and I promise to be true. Vivian, you're everything to me. My life and my breath." His brows furrowed, and a tear slid down his cheek. The reverend then addressed Vivian.

She, with tears on her eyes, said her commitment vows. "With devotion and long-lasting love, I stand before you, Jathrow. I don't remember a time when you weren't in my heart. I love you, Jathrow, today and all of our allowed tomorrows."

Sniffles were head all over the church.

Reverend Paul said, "Who gives this woman?"

David stepped closer and said, "We, her best friends, Richard Sr., Ty, and I do with her daughter Jacey." He then stepped aside, taking his place in the groom's lineup.

Jathrow's chin quivered as he willed back his built-up emotions. The reverend continued with their vows. He watched as Vivian struggled, and a single tear slid down her face. Jathrow reached for his handkerchief and lifted her veil to dab her face. Her emerald green eyes were larger and soft. He mouthed, "I love you." Then he took her hands.

Reverend Paul asked, "Is there anyone to oppose this marriage?" The room was in total silence. Finally, the reverend asked for their rings. He held them up and said, "The round circle means no end, and they're a symbol of each other being eternally connected." He nodded for Jathrow to slip the ring on her left ring finger and then nodded for Vivian to do the same on Jathrow's left ring finger. The reverend gazed at both Vivian and Jathrow and said, "I now pronounce you husband and wife." He broke into a smile. "Jathrow, you may kiss your bride."

As if in slow motion, Jathrow lifted the veil. He bent and lightly touched her glossed lips, as though Vivian was porcelain and would break. She pressed harder and momentarily he responded, fully covering his mouth with hers. The crowd cheered and howled.

Reverend Paul raised his arms again, quieting the crowd and announced, "In one hour, the reception of the newly married couple, Jathrow and Vivian Mowey, is to be held at the cottage. Everyone is invited." He cleared his throat. "For those wanting to partake in communion before attending, please stay seated." He then offered the bread and wine blessings to Jathrow and Vivian, saying, "This is the beginning of your new life together."

After the bread and wine, Jathrow and Vivian departed.

The BMW dragged tin cans and held a big Just Married sign anchored on the back. Everyone from town took their time and honked. Some shouts of congratulations were heard.

As the couple entered the doorway to the cottage, Jacey yelled, "Uncle Jathrow, it's customary to carry the bride over the threshold."

Jathrow wickedly said, "We can't break tradition now, can we?" He winked and smiled down at his bride and whisked a blushing Vivian in his arms and stepped inside the cottage. Vivian wrapped her arms around him, and they locked lips. Soon hand in hand, they admired the cottage changes.

Within the hour, more people arrived; they were escorted and seated. David in white tux and gloves ushered in the newlyweds and saw that they were served first. The music flowed in a low variety.

Richard Sr. with raised glass, clinked, and then walked on to the dance floor. He raised his glass higher in a toast and said, "Jathrow, welcome to the ball-and-chain club."

Four hundred people mingled, ate, and brought presents. The evening had gone well into the third hour when the band director said, "Last song of the night and its ladies choice." More pictures were snapped.

A short while later Jathrow bowed and led Vivian onto the dance floor.

Soon David and Doreen, Ty and Lillian, and Richard Sr. and Chloe joined them. The five adult friends had become closer, and their bond, stronger. Samuel and Sandra walked onto the danced floor for one last dance before leaving; the band director said, "Since you are the only folks left, this really is the last song."

The lights dimmed, and the music slowed. The three men broke arms with their wives; they wrapped their arms over each other's shoulder, forming a circle around Jathrow and Vivian. David said, "Let's pray, I thank You, Lord, for bringing us five together that day in the cafeteria of grade school and for walking with us in our adult lives. Thanks for the grace and mercy shown us and for finally getting through to Jathrow about our friend, Vivian, and may they be happy and their marriage be blessed. May we all continue to follow You." Within moments, David added, "Best friends forever."

Jathrow said, "Men, I wish to thank all of you for your patience and guidance throughout this journey."

Richard Sr. razzed, "Any plans for a honeymoon?"

Jathrow rose to the challenge, reached for a glass of OJ, and lifted it high, answering, "Yes. We have plans!"

Vivian blinked his way shyly.

Jathrow leaned in and kissed her rosy cheek. "Samuel, come here. Care to share the news?"

He stepped closer to the others and said, "As Vivian's agent, it's my proud privilege to announce her novel *Lasting Love* has sold out." He then nodded to Vivian. "The country where the novel was set, Switzerland, has sent tickets for her and her new husband to come. Of course, our Vivian will be their guest speaker. They're booked at the Main Hotel and were gifted with a cruise." He chuckled. "We'll see Vivian and Jathrow in a month or so."

Everyone cheered. Samuel slapped Jathrow on the back and moved with him several steps and privately said, "Walk with me."

Jathrow nodded and strolled into the kitchen. Samuel said, "Now that we both are married, I want to clear up a matter. The ring in which I gave Vivian was a token of possibilities. I had hinted, but never officially proposed. Vivian, from our beginning, spoke of you, and I knew you would always stand between us. But, Jathrow, when I met Sandra Hill, my love,

I understood exactly how Vivian felt. Loving is so deep." He cleared his throat. "Man to man, Jathrow, don't ever hurt her. Vivian is special."

Richard Sr. stood in the kitchen's doorway and heard what Mr. Gee said. He walked near the men. "Jathrow, that goes double from all your friends. Be kind, faithful, and loving. Be slow to anger and quickly forgive always." He chuckled. "A happy wife is a happy life."

19

The last band member left, yet Jathrow twirled a willing Vivian around in a waltz. Their eyes locked; they were captured in a world all their own. Jathrow dipped Vivian. After the dance, they headed toward their four friends and their wives, who were clapping. They listened as they were bid a final good night and a safe farewell.

He tenderly said to her, "Walk with me. Let's stroll on the beach and feel the sand in our toes."

Vivian nodded, not noticing the cold, but patted his hand and said with a blush, "Only a short walk, my love."

Jathrow's heart leaped; he paused in front of her, dropped a kiss, and with raised eyebrows, asked, "What did you have in mind, wife?"

Vivian's shades of pink darkened. She point toward the cottage's bedroom. She reached on tiptoe, touched his chest, and asked, "Have you seen our suite?"

Jathrow's blue eyes widened as he responded, "No."

He picked her up and wiggled his eyebrows, saying, "I thought you might be too tired for a romp in the hay."

Vivian jerked his hand. "And what were you thinking?" She unbuttoned the top of his tuxedo shirt and blew on his neck; then she unbuttoned another. She ran her fingers the length and kissed his chest. She raised her head and glanced into those dark blue eyes, and breathed, "My husband, Jathrow, I've waited for you so."

He without hesitating turned from the direction of the beach and opened the back door. He closed it with his foot. Jathrow slowly entered the bedroom and sat her on the edge of his gifted king-sized bed. With one quick swish action he had the rose petals on the floor. And in a husky voice, said, "Come, Vivian, my love, lay with me."

Vivian stood, steadying her legs. "Give me a few minutes, and I'll join you, my love."

Jathrow lit a few candles. Then shirtless and barefooted, he walked to the wide bedroom window and looked at the gold band around his finger. It was so small and yet the symbol was huge. He glanced out and thought, *Why am I so giddy and nervous? This isn't my first rodeo, but, ah, it's Vivian.* Jathrow breathed in deep, calming him, and admired the beauty surroundings the cottage of its gardens and fir and pine trees. He could only imagine how Vivian felt the first time she saw the cottage and its beautiful gardens nestled in the edge of the forest and then when she discovered the private beach. *I'm home!*

He leaned against the window frame, turned, and smiled as Vivian entered the room. He let out a low wolf whistle. On her feet were light feather-looking slippers showcasing her bright pink–painted toenails. He watched Vivian grace the room in a magnificent sheer blush pink long length silky gown with a sheer matching robe latched at her waist. He watched her blush. Vivian fluffed the pillows and placed them behind her head where she carefully pulled the satiny sheet around her. She licked her glossed lips, patted the bed, and in a low wispy whisper, breathed, "Promise me, Jathrow, until death do us part."

He slowly walked over to the bedside, touched her face, and stole a kiss. He slid to his knee and deepened the kiss. She wrapped her arms around him, breathing in his manly scent. She then placed her hands in his free flowing thick blond hair and whispered, "I've always loved you."

He without delay eased onto the bed, his arm muscles rippling, and leaned over her. He said while gazing into her beautiful green eyes, "Me too. Only I didn't know it for a long time, but I pledge forever, my love, in this life and the next." They kissed. The candles flickered when he rolled on his side and touched her robe fastener. She gasped, "Jathrow, I'm not like your other women."

The corners of his mouth slid upward, his blue eyes twinkled, and he said, "No, you certainly aren't." He bent his lips to hers and continued.

Vivian shuddered then edged her shaky hand lower and rested on his tuxedo trouser button.

He thumbed her soft shoulder. Her straps fell.

He beheld her beauty and nuzzled her neck displaying tiny kisses, whispering, "My love, I want to do this right and slow."

She snuggled closer.

They spent the night in much passion and promise.

The sun peeked through the window. Jathrow stirred and yawned. "Vivian, what time do we leave for Switzerland?" He reached out, but she was gone. He sat up and the sheet folded across his waist. He rubbed his eyes, then looked at his ring finger and smiled.

She peered through the doorway holding two cups of hot coffee. "We leave in two and a half hours. Why?" Wiggling her brows, she asked, "Did you have something else in mind, my husband?"

Jathrow joined her at the small table and thanked her for the coffee. He took a quick sip and sat the mug down. He placed a hand in her red bobbed hair and said, "I'll never tire of you, Vivian. You're everything to me. Thanks for taking pity on me and saying yes to being my wife."

Vivian moved and sat on his lap. He placed his arms around her. She ran her hands through his lengthy hair and said, "We both have a lot to be thankful for." She leaned in and licked his lips.

He lifted an eyebrow and asked, "Are you sure there's time to pack and arrive at the airport?"

She nibbled his ear and whispered, "We can always take the next flight."

Jathrow inhaled and slid his arm around her waist. "You have your speaking engagement. You've worked hard for these honors."

She nibbled his ear again.

But he held her firm and said, "We better leave now, or we won't make the next flight either."

For a moment, Vivian lingered. She felt his manly heat and was gripped with his sincerity and love. She stood and stepped back and said, "Okay, but watch out for tonight when we are alone in our honeymoon suite and wherever we are for the rest of our lives."

Jathrow bit his lip as he fingered his gold wedding ring. The corners of his mouth lifted, and his blue eyes locked with her green eyes as she winked. He replied, "My tiger, Vivian, I'll follow you to the ends of the earth and back. I'll be yours for as long as you'll have me."

She reached for Jathrow's hands and placed her small hands in his. She said, "Let's begin in prayer." Together in prayer, they assured before

God their commitments once again to each other and without question they had found each other and trust.

Jathrow touched her cheek. "I never believed there could be an us." He swung her around. "What a rare treasure you are, Mrs. Mowey."

She nodded and nuzzled his neck, saying, "My husband, my friend."

❧❦❧

Jathrow said, "The cab is here." He bowed. "You're public waits. As I, for the rest of my life."

Vivian smiled and reached for his hand and gave it a squeeze. He opened the door, and in silence, they locked the cottage and placed the key under the yellow flowerpot. He motioned for the cabbie to load their luggage. He slid in the cab after Vivian.

At the airport, they found the waiting lines weren't long, and the flight seating arrangement placed them in first class. But the stewards were a bit flirty toward Jathrow for Vivian's taste. Jathrow tightened his grip on Vivian's arm and smiled.

Vivian said, "Dear, do you think our friends will continue their monthly card games. If so, will you attend? I hear the ladies meet up with David's wife and go shopping and eat out. Sounds like fun to me, a win-win."

"Ah, Vivian, our new life together I'm sure will take on many turns. And I think joining the men's monthly card game could be fun, if not interesting. Beside it will be nice to beat the famous Richard Sr."

❧❦❧

Now back in Virginia, Richard Sr. and Ty were laughing as they hung their coats and hats on the entry rack. David said, "Come on in."

They took their seats around the card table, and David brought the platter of tier sandwiches in and offered each man to help himself. The doorbell dinged. Ty and Richard Sr. glanced at each other and then back at David. He wore a wide grin and said, "Ty, grab another chair. I think Samuel is here." The doorbell dinged again. David rushed to answer the door. "Hello, Samuel. Glad you could make it tonight for our monthly card game." David hung his coat and hat on the entry rack. He motioned Samuel into the makeshift game room.

Ty clapped Samuel on the back and said, "You're among friends. Glad you could join us."

Richard said, "Samuel, we play seven cards rule. Meet me, the champion. Just warning ya."

Ty said, "Come sit here by me."

David held out the OJ and offered each a glass. He handed a soft cloth over to Ty to sup up the overflow drippings.

Richard blurted, "How about the dainty fancy sandwiches. I'll take a few." He turned and handed several to Samuel.

David set his drink down and placed two tier sandwiches on his plate. After taking a sip, he said, "Richard Sr., haven't you shuffled and reshuffled those cards enough?" David pounded the table. "Ready, men, to take Richard Sr. down." The room became silent.

Richard Sr. brown eyes sparkled as he watched each man surrender.

The next game of cards was the same, and so was the next set. David refilled the men's glasses with the specialty drink and added more sandwiches to the platter. He took his seat and said, "Richard Sr., when Jathrow joins us, you'll be toast. No one has ever beaten him." David looked in Samuels's direction saying, "Even as we were kids sitting in the grade school's lunchroom, Jathrow won. We never played for money, but Jathrow did collect a lot of our peanut butter and jelly sandwiches."

The men laughed.

Ty said, "Remember when we bought our lunch at school on hotdog day and he ate his and all three of ours?"

Samuel said, "Has Jathrow always strived at winning?"

Richard Sr. nodded. "You could say that. From a very young age, he wanted to be successful. We all studied with Jathrow. Even though a clown, he took education very seriously."

David cleared his throat. "Jathrow was the glue that held me together after my folks were killed. He never mentioned he was the source that spoke to Doreen and informed her on what happened." He clasped his hands and stared at Samuel. He said, "When Jathrow left, our Virginia part of us were lost. We each made a pact to stay friends no matter what." He chuckled. "Some of us even tried to date Vivian, but she made it clear, we were only friends. She was the one who made arrangements for all of us to go to LA for Jathrow's law graduation. We knew she was sweet on him, but we didn't dare say a word."

Samuel nodded. "When I met Vivian and became her agent and friend, she talked a lot about him. Sadly, most of her words were of disappointment. I think because he never was honest from the beginning of his feelings for her."

Richard Sr. said, "The day she mentioned marrying the doctor surprised us all. And, well, let's say it whirlwind quickly."

Ty nodded and added, "We all thought Jathrow would pop up and say she couldn't marry the doctor, but we also thought he was a no-show."

Samuel screeched, "He came?"

David thundered, "He did, but he only watched from a distance and, after the I do's, ran to the corner store to finish watching her departure with the good doctor. Jathrow later said he wasn't well off enough or reliable as a study man for her." He sighed.

Richard Sr. stated, "Much later after the doctor's death, Jathrow came back for an annual business event and short vacation. Things between our Vivian and Jathrow heated up, and our hopes were up, and then things went all wrong. It's taken all of us to plan and work unknowingly with Vivian and Jathrow to get them together."

Ty said, "When you offered her a ring, well, we all held our breath."

David said, "I was glad when Sandra Hills came to town."

"Hello, men. Did I hear my name?"

The four men stood and a blushing Samuel hugged his wife.

David said, "Mrs. Sandra Gee, you certainly did hear us speak about how wonderful it is that you came to Virginia and met Samuel. It's nice to have extended friends." David walked over to his wife and kissed her cheek.

Doreen said, "Honey, any luck at cards tonight?"

David placed an arm around his wife and moaned, "No. None of us had any luck at cards tonight. It was the usual—Richard Sr. won."

Richard Sr. did a quick victory dance.

Ty said, "Doreen, perhaps next month when Jathrow's back from honeymooning, he'll take the championship of card winning."

Everyone in the room laughed, but Richard Sr. His brow was scrunched as he let out a held breath.

David and Doreen went to the door to bid everyone a good night and good-bye. David said, "Samuel, you're one of us now. Card game next month, same place and time." He clapped him on the back and kissed Sandra on the cheek. Arm in arm with Doreen, David watched as Samuel helped Sandra into his Buick. Richard Sr. waved at them before entering his Cadillac.

Ty was wearing a broadened smile as he swung behind the wheel of his new panel white truck.

Doreen touched David's chest. "Want me to make coffee?"

David bent down and gave his wife a lingering kiss. Then as he raised his head, brown eyes twinkling wickedly, he said, "Not tonight, my love." He swept her up in his arms and carried her to their bedroom. With only the moonlight filtering in, David breathed, "After all these years, Doreen, I love you so. So much more than the day we married." He bent his head, and their breath mingled. He leaned in and whispered, "Bed with me?"

Doreen in raspy voice said, "Turn down the bed covers, and I'll be right back." She wiggled.

But David's arms tightened, and he walked to their bed. Their kiss lingered. Then an unexpected girlie giggle escaped her. "I loved you the first moment you stole my ball and jacks at school on lunch break."

David said, "You remember? We were only in fifth grade."

"Shush, darling." Doreen placed her hands on his chest and said, "I'm waiting."

The room went silent but for the sheets rustling.

Family-Used OJ Recipe

10–12 oranges
1 qt. homemade or store-bought vanilla ice cream
1/16 tsp. vanilla extracts
1 cup ginger ale
4–6 mint leaves

- Squeeze 10 to 12 oranges into 2 qt. pitcher adding 1/16 tsp. vanilla extract. Chill.

- When ready to serve, lace vanilla ice cream into freshly chilled orange juice, then add 1 cup ginger ale. Pour on 4 to 6 oz. glasses, and place a leaf of chocolate, green, or mint leaf on top. Enjoy!

www.ingramcontent.com/pod-product-compliance
Lightning Source LLC
Chambersburg PA
CBHW060421260626
47161CB00005B/1733